TALES FROM THE GUILD WORLD TOUR

Edited by Ocean Tigrox

Co-edited by Madison Keller, George Squares, and MikasiWolf

Tales from the Guild: World Tour

Production Copyright © 2018 FurPlanet Productions

Cover illustration by Lando
furaffinity.net/user/sicklyhypnos

Cover design by George Squares

Published by FurPlanet Productions
Dallas, TX
www.FurPlanet.com

ISBN 978-1-61450-437-5
First Edition Trade Paperback 2018

TABLE OF CONTENTS

What is the Furry Writers' Guild?

Foreword

What is the Furry Writers' Guild?

The Furry Writers' Guild aims to support, inform, elevate, and promote quality anthropomorphic fiction and its creators. Since its origin in 2010, the organization has worked with writers to provide information to help them grow and learn. The membership requirements are simple and, although there are benefits to being a Guild member, many of the resources provided are there for both member and non-member authors.

The Guild is not just for writers, though. It aims to be a resource for readers, as well. With this anthology, you can see a showcase of some of our members at their best.

Furry or not, author or reader, writers of fiction or nonfiction, there is something for all within the guild. Our forums and online chats welcome all comers, and we hope that you will find something to help, something to delight, and a community of which you can be a part.

Find out more at furrywritersguild.com

Proceeds from the sale of this anthology will go back to helping fund the Guild. Thank you for your contribution!

FOREWORD

There's so much diversity on this big blue rock we live on. From vast societies scattered across the globe, to simple differences in slang from one province to the next. We each know so much about where we've grown up and the places we've travelled, but so little compared to everything still to see. There are countless stories happening around the globe and this anthology is an attempt to use those locations, those societies and those experiences to craft our own creative tales around them.

Although these stories are works of fiction, I hope they'll encourage you. Whether it inspires you to explore more of what's out there, travel somewhere you've never gone, take some time to learn more about the history of where you live, or even find out more about what's happening on the other side of the planet, remember that all this can lead to creativity and inspiration in your own works. Never take your own life and experiences for granted or for something mundane. Always be looking to add more to your own life story.

SHE WHO EATS

Frances Pauli

TERNATE, INDONESIA

The boat railing pitched again, making the Molucca Sea a diagonal slash of blue and turning Kit's stomach inside out. She clenched both paws around the wood and closed her eyes tight against the vertigo, the sense that her world was toppling overboard.

Ms. Jones, we regret to inform you that your mother has passed.

Kit swallowed bile and pushed the echo of the letter to the back of her mind. *Stay in the moment, Kit.* She needed to keep it together. The wood felt smooth under her pads, the sea matched the blue of the sky, and on the horizon, the rocky cone of Gamalama crowned her destination.

The last place she wanted to go. The worst reason to be arriving.

"Miss Jones?" The tiger captain she'd hired in Sofifi called to her from the wheel. His striped arm waved, and Kit reluctantly released the railing and staggered toward the rear deck.

"How much longer?"

"Minutes." The captain pointed a curving black claw toward the volcanic island. "This is not a place for city kitties to holiday."

"Trust me, it's not a holiday." She'd have much rather stayed in Jakarta, where she kept a comfortable apartment in a city full of the happy memories of her childhood. Despite the lawyer's insistence, Kit knew all she'd find in Ternate was the sting of her mother's abandonment. She swiped her long tail against the deck, accidentally soiling the calico fur with salt water and filth. Kit scowled and flicked it irritably in an attempt to dislodge the dirt. "I've no interest in staying a moment longer than necessary."

I'll be back for holidays, Kitten. It won't be forever.

She closed her eyes and heard her mother's voice whispering empty promises for the thousandth time. It *had* been forever, in the end. Every apologetic letter, every well-intentioned excuse did nothing to erase the fact. *Mom chose Ternate. She picked this place over me.*

"Three hours to sail back once you send word," the captain's baritone growled, dragging Kit into the present.

"You're not staying?" Her whiskers tightened as the scent of the docks, thick and full of fish, reached her nostrils. Her stomach threatened to evacuate her morning meal of fruit and synthetic tuna.

"Things you'll have to do will take time. More than you believe, I think. Enough time to earn another fare or two."

"I was hoping to be quick." She flicked her tail against the back of her legs and pressed the tips of her claws against her pants leg. "I'm not here to sightsee."

"These things take a while," the tiger insisted. "You'll see. Island animals don't move like city animals, don't do anything like city animals." He shuddered, prompting her curiosity despite her intentions.

"What does that mean?"

"Island life is slow," he said. "But Ternate is different. Some say, in the shadow of Gamalama, they still eat the meat." He grimaced, showing a mouthful of yellow-stained fangs.

"That's ridiculous." Kit sniffed and then pressed a paw pad over her nose. She mumbled, trying not to let the smell in. "My mother wouldn't have stayed if they did."

The salty odor only became a thicker presence as they neared the shore. The blurred line between land and sea clarified into a row of shabby buildings on stilts. Docks projected between these at random intervals, and behind it all, the green slope of Gamalama lifted toward her peak.

"Someone's waiting for you." The tiger maneuvered his craft toward the widest of the docks.

A crowd had gathered: a cluster of the short reptilian locals that she recognized from the few photos her mother had sent home. Monitor lizards. The animals which made their home on the island wore loose garments that matched their black and yellow scales, scant clothing designed for an active life in the tropical setting.

Their natural lack of fur had made Kit twitchy when she was younger. Now, it showcased how different Ternate was and caused her to doubly question her mother's decision to live there. Research was one thing. Mrs. Jones had always put her career first. But to live like this… surrounded by half naked reptiles?

Kit meant to close her eyes to will the approaching island and its colorful population out of existence. Instead, a flash of white caught her attention. Her eyes were drawn to a larger motion, a taller figure among the mob.

"Flat head cat." The tiger grinned and then turned his head and spat onto the deck of his boat. "He'll take care of your business."

"Who is he?" Kit hardly had to squint to see the crowd now. The wash of colors solidified into individual animals. The cat in the middle of the lizards wore a white suit and hat. He stood tall and out of place among the shorter islanders.

"Marshal," the tiger said. "Ternate liaison to all of Indonesia."

"Sounds important." Kit narrowed her eyes and made out a pelt of gold beneath the white suit.

"Not really." The captain laughed and spit again. "He

might have money, but he's got no power in the jungle. On these slopes, it's the little *Bomoh* who runs the show. That one, city kitties would do good to steer clear of."

"The shaman or Marshal?"

"Yes!" A striped fist pounded against the ship's wheel, and the tiger captain laughed until it turned into a growl. "Both of *them*, and the island too. City kitty should have stayed at home."

"Maybe so." Kit watched the dock grow, the lizards milling, and the single, white-clad cat prowling among them. She inhaled the aroma of salt and fish, bracing against her stomach's complaint and wishing she'd been able to do what the captain suggested. Wishing she'd stayed in Jakarta.

Mrs. Jones specifically requested that you come to Ternate.

Her mother's last wishes had dragged her to this island, and despite ten years of abandonment, resentment, and anger, Kit had answered without hesitation. She'd obeyed like a good kitten, as if she'd even *had* a mother for the last decade.

She sighed and swiped her tail back and forth. "I didn't really have a choice."

***

"Kittitas Jones, I'd know you anywhere." The cat in the white suit had a broad face and a wide, friendly smile. He extended a paw to help Kit from the boat, and used his other to tilt his hat for her in a remarkably courteous, if old-fashioned, gesture.

"How is that?" She took his paw and allowed him to steady her on the swaying dock. "Have we met?"

"No." His smile only stretched further, showing white teeth. Perhaps the island food was better than in Sofifi. Kit's belly warmed at the thought, but the cat in white ruined it with his next words. "Your mother has shown me many photographs. Your face is known in town, though of course the images could not fully convey how lovely you are in person."

"My mother…"

"I'm very sorry for your loss." His smile dimmed, but not enough for Kit to believe his words. He still clutched her paw in his, and his eyes flashed as if the sun had gone out, as if they stood alone in the dark.

"Who are you?" She pulled her paw away and braced herself against the dock's movement by stepping wider and counterbalancing with her tail. "The captain said—oh."

The boat had already pulled away from the dock, making more distance than she'd have expected in a few short moments of conversation. Kit flattened her ears and watched her contact shrinking into the sea. The tiger had assured her she could send a telegraph as soon as she was ready to leave, promising he could return within a few hours.

She still felt the weight of his abandonment as an ill omen.

"My name is Jake." The flat-headed cat had removed his white hat. He held it in front of his chest now, and his expression had turned serious. "Jake Marshal, and I am sorry for your loss, Kitten, but not so sorry that you've come at last to Ternate."

"It's Kit." She glared at him. Only her mother called her Kitten. "And I plan on leaving as quickly as possible."

"A tragedy." He grinned again, showed her white teeth, and held out his elbow. "But not unexpected. Shall we?"

"Shall we what?" The sea swirled, conspiring against her and tossing her toward Jake Marshal. Kit kept her stance, tried to grab his elbow casually, without giving away how much she needed him for balance.

"I've been charged with helping you complete your business here. You wish to finish as soon as possible, but perhaps we should get the viewing over with first?"

"The viewing." She'd known, of course, that she'd have to see the body. It still hadn't felt real until that moment. Her mother was dead, lain out here in the middle of the sea with only the lizards for company. Kit allowed Jake Marshal to lead her from the dock to the land. She moved automatically, numb, her head full of her mother's voice.

If you'd only come to visit, Kitten. You might understand.

But she never would, not if the volcano towering overhead crumbled to dust, or the shacks around them turned to gold and the skies rained synthetic fish to drown out the stink of real flesh. She'd never forgive her mother, and now, she'd have to face her knowing there would be no answers, no explanation ever.

"Kitten?" The face of Jake Marshal resolved into focus. He peered down at her, worry pressing his ears to either side of his wide head. "Sorry, *Kit*. Are you well?"

Her fugue had dragged them to a stop in the middle of a rough dirt avenue lined with shabby buildings. They'd walked inland far enough that the stilts had vanished, and the street angled up at a gentle but obvious slope toward the jungles at the base of Gamalama. Though the smell of the sea lingered, a new aroma swept inland, sweet and pungent and oddly familiar.

Kitten.

She shook her head and swiped her tail high enough above the road to keep it from any further sullying. "Sorry about that. Lost in thought."

"Would you rather wait?"

"No." She wanted this over as quickly as possible. "It's fine. I'm fine."

The crowd from the dock had dispersed while they spoke, and now the reptilian locals continued about their business, readying outbound crates and pushing carts and cargo from the dock to the shops along the street. They pointed long snouts at Kit and blinked round eyes surrounded by bright yellow scales. When she glanced in their direction, the faces turned quickly away, but as soon as her eyes moved on, she knew their attention fixed back on her, on Jake Marshal holding her arm, leading her toward her mother's body.

"I'm fine." She asserted it, louder this time.

"They don't mean to be rude," Jake said. "They're just very curious."

"I suppose my mother showed them my picture as well?"

16

"Oh yes."

"Well that's just great." Kit lashed her tail against her legs and pressed her claw tips into her pads. So many eyes watched her, and all of them knew who she was. All of them knew her mother better than she did.

Jake tried again. "Your mother—"

She pulled her arm from his and stepped a pace to the side. "Just take me to her."

"Very well." He bowed low, dragged his hat close to the dusty road, and straightened without taking a step. His stance shifted just enough to notice if you she were really looking.

She caught the tension in the new set of his shoulders and she saw the tip of his tail twitch.

Ahead of them, one of the lizards had taken center stage. He posed beneath an arch of rough wood, behind which the city faltered and the jungle swooped in to take the place of civilization. He stood the same as the rest, about chest high to Kit, and his scales were black over most of his body, brilliant yellow in the stripes running over his eyes. Still, nothing about him felt the same as the islanders wandering between Ternate's buildings.

This one wore a long, emerald green sarong and a crown of spiky feathers. He raised one arm straight into the air. Kit would have known exactly who he was even if his gesture hadn't silenced the movements of his people. The shaman held something in his claws. He shook it and it rattled, chasing away the echo of the lizard's hissing with a sound like bones clattering, like the tumbling of stones down the side of Gamalama.

"It's okay," Jake Marshal whispered. He'd sidled up to Kit again, and one of his paws settled against her shoulder. "Pikau is our Bomoh."

"A shaman?"

"Of a sort, yes."

"That explains my mother's interest."

"She fought for them," Marshal's voice adopted a defensive note. "Went to the city many times to argue on their behalf.

Because of her, the lizards are allowed to keep their ways, if only on this corner of the island."

The shaman rattled again and shouted something in a language built of hissing sounds and the clacking of teeth. His voice refused to pick an octave. It warbled high and low at turns and echoed all the way past them as if he spoke to the sea.

Kit's fur lifted. Her whiskers twanged against the sounds, the rattling, and the soft rumbling in the distance that might have been the volcano. Her tail twitched a warning, and she remembered the tiger captain's words. Only minutes after he'd dropped Kit off, she stood in the street with Jake Marshal, facing this Pikau, when he'd suggested she steer clear of them both.

"He welcomes you to Ternate," Jake assured her. "And expresses the island's sorrow for your mother."

Kit tried to smile. Her whiskers were too tight, and she feared she showed more fang than the lizard would appreciate. "Thank you."

The shaman shrieked and leaped into the air. Kit flinched into Jake Marshal's side. A wrong choice, but something that happened too fast to remedy. Jake's scent filled her nostrils, and her body tensed, reacting to the proximity of the attractive tom.

The Bomoh jumped so high that the very tip of his tail became the only thing anchoring him to the island. He threw up both his arms this time, and when he fell back to earth, he flung the rattle to his feet.

It shattered against the street.

"It's okay." Marshal repeated. "It's just…"

"I'm not a child." Kit cringed from him. She kept her eyes on the lizard shaman, but now that his tantrum had ended, he seemed to deflate. His claws dragged against the street, etching something around the broken instrument. Once he'd finished scratching, however, he turned without ceremony and stalked away, deep into the jungle.

"Come." Jake said. "This way."

"After *him*?"

Jake Marshal stuffed his white hat back over his ears and

shrugged. "Of course."

He marched away without looking back. Kit hesitated, but only until the nosy locals returned to their business. Then she hurried after, and when she reached the spot where Pikau had thrown his fit, Kit kept her eyes on the ground. She found the remains of the shaman's toy, a burst gourd and a scattering of teeth.

If the marks he'd scratched in the dirt meant anything, Kit couldn't guess what. She stepped over them, reluctant for some reason to disturb the detritus. Needle teeth in the dust, shards of gourd and one larger fang that couldn't have come from a lizard.

Kit didn't want to know whose tooth that was any more than she cared to see her mother's body. Today, the universe didn't seem to give a damn what she wanted. Gamalama rumbled in the distance, Jake Marshal continued in the wake of the shaman lizard, and Kit had no choice but to lift her tail high and follow.

***

They'd laid her mother inside their temple. The island's buildings grew less modern the farther they wandered from the shoreline. The walls shrank, and eventually most of the houses existed primarily as roofs held aloft by sparse poles and the occasional privacy screen. The temple proved the grandest of these structures by far, sitting atop a shelf in the island landscape like a huge, open-aired vulture waiting to pounce on the town below.

Or maybe that was her mood talking.

Kit stared up at it and tried to think of a reason not to keep going. The jungle encroached on civilization here. Dense green foliage replaced the walls, and the steady music of Indonesian birds and insects played her mother's funeral dirge. A merrier sound than Kit would have expected, but then, the decorations heaped around and up the temple walkway suggested one hell of a party.

A long stair wound from the street to the temple, lined with a rugged rail made of wood that had not been hewn in any uniform fashion. Garlands of flowers twined over and under the railing, and the blooms spilled onto the steps. The air filled with a sweet smell—a fresh but also spicy aroma that Kit couldn't quite pin down. There were bundles of bright cloth amid the flowers, too, and strings of polished stone, boxes, plates of food. A treasure lining the pathway to her dead mother.

Kit focused on Marshal, on the only thing that seemed even slightly familiar to her in Ternate. "What is all this?"

"The islanders show their appreciation for She Who Eats."

The accent was perfect, which threw her for a moment, since Jake Marshal's lips had not moved. He stood beside her as mute as the flowers, and her answer had come from the stairway. His eyes narrowed though, and Kit followed his gaze to find the lizard, Pikau, had reappeared facing them from three steps up the climb. Eye to eye now.

"She Who Eats?" Kit blurted, and the reptilian eyes blinked.

"It is how they know your mother," Jake whispered. "The name the locals gave her."

"Her title," Pikau corrected. "She Who Eats honored Ternate with her life. Now we honor her in death."

"It's an old custom." Jake Marshal explained away the shaman's severe tone and earned a narrowed gaze from Pikau. The lizard's tongue slid out and down, forked at the end and reaching near to the ground. After descending, it retracted so slowly that Kit found herself mesmerized, watching the pink tips below the scowling face. The deliberate slowness of the gesture felt like a reprimand. This time, Kit suspected it was not meant for her.

"Come, daughter of She Who Eats." Pikau turned and darted up the stairway, moving more like a snake than a lizard. His body flowed around the bends, and his stout but generous tail whiplashed through the air behind him.

"It's okay." Jake repeated it like a mantra.

From the stairway above, however, Pikau's voice reprimanded again, sharp and lilting, this time in the language of the lizards.

Kit allowed Jake's paw at her elbow, and they climbed together behind the priest, stepping gingerly over the offerings that the locals had heaped upon her mother. *She Who Eats.* Kit couldn't reconcile the words with the cat she knew, with the upright, formal queen who'd raised her affectionately from a distance. She closed her eyes, breathed, and let Jake's grip steady her progress.

"What is that smell?" A sweet burning filled her nose. Her stomach rumbled.

"Ternate and her sister are known as the Spice Islands," Jake answered. "For many years, her forests were plundered for the clove and the nutmeg."

"And now?"

"Now we eat very well here." His grin flashed, drawing Kit out of her musings, from dark thoughts and regrets. The flat-headed cat had a jovial spirit, and even in grief and confusion, Kit found it infectious. His fangs were white and sharp. His eyes flashed like his smile. "Yes. We eat very well in Ternate."

"Is that why they called her She Who Eats?"

Jake Marshal tripped over the next stair. They both teetered, gripped each other for balance, and ended up muzzle to muzzle. Kit smelled it on him too: a warm comfort of spice. His eyes flashed, and he whispered, "Perhaps."

Her whiskers tightened, twanged with the proximity of the tom, with his scent, with his presence. He'd offered no real answer, and she suspected he knew it. But she allowed him to hold her for a breath longer, a warm moment, before they continued their climb. Her curiosity won again a few more steps up. "She never told me anything about this place. The letters all just asked me to come, asked how I was and how soon I could get away."

"She missed you always."

"Not enough to come home."

The closer they drew to the temple, the more the stairways overflowed. Kit had to climb over the offerings now, to wade through flowers that reached her hock, and carry her tail unnaturally high for her mood.

"Perhaps her work here was more important than you imagine?"

"More important than her family?" Kit flicked her tail against the railing. "Yes. That's exactly what I think."

"I'm not sure you understand." Jake reached the last step, stood on the temple platform beneath a woven roof, and offered her a paw she suddenly didn't care to take. "Come."

She shrugged off his assistance and stepped up. The temple occupied the entire level space at the edge of the spice forest. The walls were knee-high plank barriers that did nothing to keep out the insects and birds but left a stunning view of the sea on two sides of the building. Rough poles supported the frond roof, and flower garlands hung from the lattice between them.

A red bird perched on one beam, its head tilting to one side when Kit entered the temple. A round orange eye examined her, and a sharp avian alert announced that her attention was fixed, pointedly away from the reason for her visit: the funeral bed occupying the center of the rectangular space.

A trail of offerings led the way, but Kit's steps refused to follow it. Her neck craned in all ways but forward. She spied a green beetle on the railing, a place to the right where the garland had snapped and the flowers scattered across the floor.

"Kit?" Jake's voice softened and purred.

"I'm fine."

"You keep saying that." He took her elbow and eased her back into position.

The lizard shaman knelt beside the platform, his feather crown now removed. If he cared that they'd arrived at last, it didn't show. He'd twisted his head and laid his pointed muzzle across the funeral shroud. His long neck stretched out baring a smooth yellow throat. His yellow eyes streamed with tears, and his tail curled protectively around his body.

Kit gaped at the pose, the submission of it. Why? Pikau ruled Ternate. Everything about the Bomoh was a claim to power. Why did she suddenly feel adrift, as if the temple floor rocked with the sea, and the green wall of jungle swayed and shook?

She stumbled forward, pulled by the intimacy of the lizard's posture. His throat tightened. A low hissing rose to the beams above. But it was *her* mother lying there. Kit looked now, had to look, with that yellow throat vibrating everywhere else.

They'd piled mats beneath the body, heaped cushions, pillows and gorgeous printed fabrics there for her mother to rest on. Mrs. Jones reclined atop the mountain of comfort, shrouded in veils of mosquito netting and looked for all intents and purposes as if she were having a nap.

Kit circled her and stepped well out of reach of the priest's tail should the hissing escalate. She approached her mother from the opposite side, and the exposed yellow throat stilled. The temple fell silent. Only an island breeze riffled the netting as soft as a whisper.

She Who Eats. Kit gazed at her mother through the veils and tried to see the change there. The soft calico fur was as tidily groomed as ever. The fluffy paws had been posed across one another over her mom's chest, a position she'd seen her use at least daily for nineteen years. Her wedding ring was gone, but Kit herself had urged the removal of it only six months after her father had left them for his European mistress.

No matter which way she tilted her head, that was her mom lying on the pile of pillows. No matter how many times she said it in her mind, no matter if she'd come to the end of the world or not, her mother was dead.

Kit pressed her eyes shut. Her ears lowered to the sides, and her tail dragged against the planks. No chance of a reunion now. No point in clinging to anger, in feeling resentment. She pricked her claws against her thighs. None of it would help her.

Nothing would bring her mother back.

If she screamed her accusations now, if she gave into the urge to rail at her mother's body, Kit was pretty sure the lizard shaman would try to tear her to pieces. Would he crush her into the dust like his rattle? Like cast off bones and teeth?

She inhaled and heard how ragged that breath was, how much it threatened to break her. Her mother dreamed behind closed eyes, whispered through tight lips, sounding just like the wind. *Kitten.* An insect hummed. Kit wept for the answers she'd never get. She cried for the fury she'd have to swallow, the rage that had devoured her for the last ten years.

She Who Eats.

Movement at her side pried her eyes wide again. Kit's fur stood at attention. Her whiskers vibrated as another low hiss erupted from Pikau's throat. Jake Marshal had crept to her side. The shaman stood erect now, his throat no longer bared and his eyes blinking away the tears that had possessed him. He hissed at Jake, Kit was sure, but the flat-headed cat paid him no heed. A warm paw slipped into hers, a living pulse beating beneath a golden pelt.

"It's okay," he said, lying whether he knew it or not. However flat his reassurance, the squeeze of his paw steadied her, even when he dropped to his knees beside her dead mother. Even when he tilted his head back and bared his throat.

Kit held to his paw and felt the life beating. She held to Jake Marshal, and let her mother's crimes fade in the hissing of the wind, the insects, and the little black-and-yellow shaman. Ternate had taken her mother from her, and in the shadow of Gamalama, Kit finally let her go.

***

"She lived here?" Kit leaned over the balcony wall and eyed the verdant slope, the strip of beach where it met the sea. "How could she afford this?"

"She Who Eats didn't have to afford anything." Jake Marshal's voice drifted through the open living area from the nook kitchen. The scent of whatever he was cooking came with his words, rich and thick and, Kit hoped, protein-heavy.

"Wait? What did you say?" She turned away from the tropical view and faced the room again. More drapery, thin cloth draped across the woven furniture. A platform that served as both bed and couch filled the majority of the space, but her mother had collected island things too. Vases and boxes and strings of shells—were these also offerings to She Who Eats?

"Come." He breezed between kitchen and lanai, carrying two plates and a lungful of delicious aroma. "You eat, I'll talk."

Kit scrambled to follow, past the vase with peacock feathers and the wall with twin fans made of some sort of local bark. She darted after Jake Marshal with her stomach in knots, and not only from the idea of a decent meal. It had been a long time since she'd allowed herself to notice a male.

The view from the lanai showed more beach and one side of Gamalama reaching down toward the sea. Her mother's home was surrounded by spice trees, the breeze adding ambiance to the meal Jake had prepared. Kit dived into a protein patty soaked in sweet sauce and tried to remember what she'd even asked him.

"You're sure we can get things in order tomorrow?" She swallowed one gulp and reached for her coconut cup, sniffing the contents. "This isn't water."

"Rum." Jake's laughter purred. "Only thing worth drinking here."

He took a bite of his own food and then leaned forward on his elbows and watched her instead.

"It's good." Kit ignored a wave of self-consciousness. She was starving. "Does mom have taurine handy or... I have some capsules in my purse."

"It's in the sauce." His eyes sparkled, reflecting the sky and sea. "Your mother's position, you see, is very important to the lizards' culture."

"Mom was a scientist." Kit sipped the rum and felt the heat instantly. "She came here to study their diet and the effects of low protein on the locals."

"But she became much more than that to the people here," he insisted. "She Who Eats is a spiritual leader, and an important part of the annual festival. Without her…"

He shook his head, left that dangling in the warm air, and stared out to sea.

"What did you mean about not affording anything?"

"She Who Eats is given everything she needs and more." Jake's gaze swung back to her. His eyes flashed. "This home and its contents will pass to her successor."

"I'm not here to make claims." Kit tightened her ears against her skull. "I don't want anything to do with her life here. I came because the letter said there were legalities that needed handling. What exactly those are, I haven't a clue. But you've no need to worry about me wanting anything that should go to the next She Who Eats."

"Not even that title?"

Kit slammed her coconut mug to the table and gaped at him. He didn't blink, didn't flinch away from the insane suggestion. "You're mad."

"There are worse things than staying in Ternate and living like a goddess." He shrugged it off and turned back to the view. "But I never thought you would accept it. I told Pikau as much before you arrived."

"You told him… Pikau wanted me to?"

"He still does." Jake refilled her rum, though the little coconut was only half empty. "Finish your meal. I want to take a walk, show you the beach."

"I've no interest in staying." Kit swallowed a bite of the sweet patty and glared at him. If he meant to help the priest convince her, to join Pikau in the crazy notion that she might take her mother's place, he had a colossal disappointment coming. "I just want to finish my business."

"The island mourns." Jake sighed and stared up toward the peaks of Gamalama. "The locals don't take business as seriously as they do ritual."

Kit gripped the edge of the table with her claws, let the tips drag over the iron. She felt like she'd stepped off the tiger's boat and landed backwards in time. There weren't supposed to be any shamans left on Ternate. This Bomoh, his rituals and the ridiculous title they'd given her mother set her teeth together and made her fur prickle and lift. Now she was stuck waiting here until the locals decided to come back to reality?

"Relax, Kit." Jake smiled and his eyes flashed. "The offices will open tomorrow. I'm sure of it. Tonight, let me show you what Ternate has to offer, yes? Let Jake give you a tour. Relax a little bit and you might just enjoy it."

Kit plucked her claw tips from the metal and felt his promise in the twanging of her whiskers. His eyes flashed. The air carried in thick spices, and the sea danced below like a diamond blanket. She swiped her long tail against her mother's deck and spoke through her fangs. "Fine."

***

Come, Kitten. Look and see.

"Mom?" Kit stumbled, reached for a low branch, and scanned the path ahead of her. "Is that you?"

A flash of calico fur danced behind the waving fronds. *Come Kitten. Hurry now.* The wind swirled the jungle, and Kit felt a presence at her back, something pushing her to run. She scrambled forward, ducking leaves and weaving between the overgrowth that made an obstacle course of the trail.

Come.

Her mother's ghost led her onward. The same voice that had once sang her to sleep now lulled her into a sense of complacency. She moved obediently, following the flashing tip of a familiar tail down the slope toward the scent of dead fish.

Here, Kitten. Look. Understand.

The trail widened at the bottom of the slope, exposing a dark stretch of beach, a midnight sky and thrashing sea below. The sand tugged at her steps, but Kit dragged her claws through it, lifted her tail and followed the shaggy shadow of her mother to the water's edge.

She Who Eats. See.

Her mother stepped into the water and it rippled and tugged at the long skirt of her island-made dress. She kept her back to Kit, but her voice sounded from all directions, from the air above and the sand below. *It's almost time.*

"Why?" Kit's voice cracked. The words had no power, no volume. She thought the things she wanted to shout, the questions, but when they fell from her lips, the sea devoured them. "Why didn't you come home?"

Look.

Her mother hunched forward and plunged her arms into the water. Her fluffy tail skimmed over the waves and her head fell back. She lifted her paws again, dripping, clutching something that flashed and wriggled.

See, Kitten.

She Who Eats held the fish high. The moon emerged from cover, lit her in a silver halo to match her prey. Her claws extended, gleaming now, pricking the fish scales and freeing thin red rivulets that dribbled over her white fur. She turned and faced Kit with a smile as familiar as a reflection.

"Mom." Kit choked on the word. The sea roared.

She Who Eats opened her mouth, curled her pink tongue, and stuffed the fish head against her fangs.

***

"Kitten?"

Kit screamed. She shook her head, pressed her eyes tight.

"Kit!"

"No. No." She opened her eyes and blinked in confusion at Jake Marshal. Memories of the night before rushed back, the walk on the beach, the dancing, and the massage that had gone a long way toward easing her frustration.

"Are you okay?" He sat up in bed, and the covers pooled

around them both. Jake's paw cupped her shoulder, as warm as the concerned look on his face. "You were screaming."

"Bad dream." She tried to smile, tried to erase the image of her mother gorging herself on a still-wiggling fish. Jake's paw brushed the fur of her shoulder and down her arm, managing to twist her thoughts to less horrid topics. His fur was golden everywhere, but he had spots... in lovely places.

"I'll make breakfast." He slid naked from under the sheets, stood and scanned about for his clothing while Kit examined his body and confirmed her memory of his markings. "Then we'll get you back to town as quick as possible."

"I really appreciate it."

He grinned and tugged his shirt over his head. "The breakfast or the quick exit?"

"Both, but that last one only because—"

"You have business to attend to." His grin stretched across his face, tempting her to delay him a little. "I know."

When he danced toward the kitchen another thought struck her. Jake Marshal was certainly comfortable in her mother's home. He'd settled into the kitchen as if he'd used it before. Kit's stomach tightened, and not just out of hunger. She flung her legs over the side of the bed and dressed.

When Jake returned with a tray, quickly, without any fumbling or searching for ingredients, Kit steeled herself. "Can I ask you something I don't really want to know?"

"Well, that's a new one." He set the tray down on the bed she'd just finished making and eyed her with his head tilted to one side and his whiskers twitching. "Shoot."

"Did you ever sleep with my mother?"

"Ahh." His ears perked back up again and he shook his wide head. "No."

"Oh thank god."

"The consort of She Who Eats died with her."

"Oh. I'm sorry." Kit suffered a flash of guilt, followed by a new storm of worry. "Wait. The paperwork said my mother's death was—"

"Heart-attack." Jake flopped down beside the tray and plucked a piece of fruit with two claws. "But the morning of her death, Sompa climbed to the top of Gamalama and jumped."

He mimed the descent with his mango slice, down, down, into the volcano.

"Seriously?" Kit tried to imagine it, to picture the dead consort who'd loved her mother so much that he couldn't live without her. Perhaps it was more than her work that kept She Who Eats away from her only child.

"It is the custom," Jake shrugged and ate the mango. "Being chosen as the partner of She Who Eats is a great honor."

"What exactly does it mean?" Kit grabbed some fruit for herself and dipped a piece of pineapple into the same sweet, taurine-laced sauce from the night before. "What did my mom do here?"

"For most of the year, the title is symbolic. She Who Eats embodies the hunger of the world. During the festival, she leads the island in its most sacred rite."

"Which is?"

"Difficult to explain to an outsider." His eyes flashed again, and he looked at Kit as if he wanted to see through her. "I'm not sure you're ready to hear it."

"Ready or not," Kit said. "I don't plan on being here any longer than it takes to get her business in order."

"Well then." Jake Marshal sighed and reached one paw to Kit's face. He trailed a claw along her jaw and purred deep in his chest. "I suppose I'll just have to explain it to you on the way."

***

"I don't believe it." Kit tugged on the door until the hinges rattled, but it remained locked. "How can they just close everything down and still stay in business?"

"The festival is more significant than business." Jake held back a few paces, watched her as if she might turn and rattle *him* next.

To be honest, it was tempting.

"I don't believe that either. All that rubbish. You're talking about the woman who raised me."

"She Who Eats partakes of the flesh so that the rest of the world doesn't have to."

"My mother was a devout vegetarian." Kit stared at the dark office window. She tried to see the reflection of Jake Marshal, but her head filled with the images from her dream. Her mother's claws around a fat silver fish. Her mother's mouth, dripping blood at the corners. How had her dream known something she hadn't?

"When she arrived in Ternate, yes. Before she understood."

"You believe this, too? You're no local, Jake Marshal." She turned back to the street, to the town he claimed was closed down. The lizards still wandered along the road. They still led their children past the dark windows and stood on street corners in little clusters as if there were something in town to do, something to see.

They're watching me. They're all here to see what I'll do next.

"My mother was a scientist, and you're certainly worldly enough, intelligent enough not to give this superstition any weight."

"I have seen enough things to know better than to dismiss something so quickly, without investigation."

"Mr. Marshal." Kit stood taller and swished her tail back and forth above the dirty sidewalk. Their spectators moved into the open. The lizard population crept forward to watch the show, and hundreds of black eyes blinked and flashed from the roadsides. "Predation was eradicated through generations of adaptation, through study and dietary modification... The very things my mother stood for. We worked for hundreds of years to remedy our need to kill one another. Our intellects evolved to understand that it is *unacceptable*. Do you mean to tell me that here in this town, the entire world's hunger is held at bay because of one sacrifice? That all our history and the combined efforts of science and philosophy mean nothing, and we'll all suddenly revert to our basest instincts if my mother doesn't run into the jungle once a year and eat a fish!"

Her voice pitched dangerously close to hysterical at the end, but the screeching of her own disbelief, paled to a whisper when his eyes flashed, when he jerked back and shook his flat head sadly. "No. Not that."

"What do you mean?" Kit whispered, caught in his expression and the sinking horror in her stomach. "Isn't that what you just told me?"

"You don't understand."

Look, Kitten. Understand.

"You've lost your mind." She backed away from him and found a locked door blocking her retreat. The crowd hissed and Jake Marshal never flinched. "You all have. My mother wouldn't condone this, would never participate in it."

"Maybe not when she arrived, but she respected the locals, and she honored their culture and beliefs."

"And you knew her better than I did?"

Jake Marshall held his tail perfectly still. He stared at her and said nothing until her whiskers twitched and she found herself longing to leap at him.

"I don't care what business my mother had here, I'm leaving. You can mail me any documents I need to sign."

"Okay." He put both paws up between them, showing his soft pink pads and an apologetic expression. "Peace?"

Kit flicked her tail against her legs and growled low in her throat.

"I know you're frustrated. Things don't work the same way here that they do in the cities."

"It's a wonder they work at all."

He smiled, tilted his head to one side, and eased his paws back down. "I tell you what, come to the feast tonight. Stay one more day, and I'll drag someone down to the office in the morning to get this handled."

"And if they're all at this festival in the damned jungle?" Kit curled her tongue against her fang tips and let her claws out. How had her mother lived like this? It just wasn't possible Mrs. Jones, scientist, intellectual calico had actually eaten meat? Even if it was only once a year.

Jake shrugged. He wore his white suit minus the hat, and though she'd seen him in it yesterday, had watched him pluck the rumpled shirt and trousers from her mother's carpet, he looked fresh and pressed as a worn stone. Smooth. He was all polish and pizzazz, and she definitely should have known better than to tangle with him.

Something about the look in his eyes, the flash that matched his teeth, gave her a sudden chill.

"Was that your job, then?"

"What?" His grin stretched, but the tail froze, his whiskers twanged still.

"You were supposed to keep me busy, keep me from leaving?" She pressed her ears as low as they would go and lashed her tail to the side. "Oh, God. Were you supposed to sleep with me, too?"

"No, Kitten. Not that."

"But everything else?" She glared at him, saw the truth of it in his sagging shoulders, heard enough answer in his silence. "You listen to me, Mr. Marshal. I don't care about the local customs, the festival, or anything my mother may or may not have done here. I'm going for a walk. When I come back, there had better be some way I can send a telegram, message my ride, and pay him to take me back to sanity as quickly as possible."

She spun away from him and marched down slope in the middle of the street. The water sparkled around the docks ahead, the volcano grumbled faintly from behind, and though Jake Marshal said nothing, made no move to stop her flight, the sidewalks hissed and shifted.

Kittitas Jones marched for the sea, surrounded by the protestations of the local lizards. She held her tail and her whiskers high, kept her focus on the docks, praying there would be a boat tied up there, a ship full of crates from Sofifi, or any boat at all. If she couldn't flag down a ride, she'd have to swallow her pride and go running back to Marshal for help, and she'd have rather eaten the stupid fish than do that.

Her stomach clenched at the thought. Well, maybe not. Kit grumbled in her throat and shook her head at no one in particular. Not a chance her mother had done it, either. No matter what Jake Marshal said. Kit scanned the empty docks and then turned a desperate gaze on the sea.

No boats in sight. No way out.

She veered toward the beach that ran below the stilts. The tide was low, and the shoreline buildings looked like wading birds, long-legged and leaning this way and that. Kit padded through the sand, weaving around moorings, under walkways and between the long stilts that kept the city above the tide.

Her steps beat a soft rhythm, *send the telegram, get off the island.* She let the mental chant drive her onward until the sand strip widened and the buildings gave up the chase. Jungle swept all the way to the beach and the sweet, overpowering scent of clove blanketed the stink of the sea.

Better. At least now she could think. Jake Marshal's words haunted her thoughts. *She honored their culture and beliefs.* That part did sound like her mom. Kit supposed it was possible, if the fish were killed painlessly, that her mother might have taken up this duty, this She Who Eats rubbish.

It doesn't mean I have to.

She slowed her stomping down to a pensive wander, let the sand warm her pads and the sun ease away some of the tension in her shoulders. Her fur amplified the tropical heat, and she pulled off her outer shirt and tied it around her waist.

The air had a softening effect here. It also made her fur bushy, so that her tail looked perpetually irritated. Or maybe that had to do with the company she'd kept. Kit sighed and swiped her tail against the sand. He had been a good time, and she couldn't deny a stab of disappointment that it wouldn't go any further.

She listened to the sea whisking up and down the shore.

She felt the sun's rays on her pelt and inhaled the spices, the salt, and even the fish. Not so bad, really. In an emergency, if proper synthetic protein weren't available, she supposed it wouldn't kill her to try it.

Look, Kitten. See.

The dream had been a little too gory for Kit's taste, but maybe her mother had been trying to explain things to her. Kit tilted her head back and glowered at the clouds. "Next time go a little easy on the blood, okay?"

"But blood is what Gamalama craves." The words came so clearly that it took Kit a moment to recognize who said it. She'd barely placed the voice when the little shaman slithered out of the jungle and onto the sand.

"Why?" She shuffled backwards, gave him a few tail length's distance. "Rituals are symbolic things. Why not make an effigy? Why not a representational feast?"

She'd paid enough attention to her mother's work to know more than the ordinary cat about indigenous customs. Her self-congratulation, however, died in Pikau's disdain.

"The world's hunger will not be held at bay by a tofu fish." He scoffed and lashed his tail purposefully between them, flinging sand up in a gritty veil. "You think we do this thing lightly, but wouldn't any of us go willingly to our deaths to keep the rest from harm?"

"I find that hard to believe."

"Then you're not as wise as your mother was."

"My mother was a biologist." Kit stamped one paw against the sand and flattened her ears. "I don't know what lies you told her, what tricks you used, but she didn't believe in this crap. Maybe she only played along to placate you."

Pikau hissed. His forked tongue slid out and back. The beach echoed the low sound, vibrated with a dozen answers to his irritation. Kit swung around, crouching, hissing in return.

The whole beach writhed black and yellow. Scaly bodies shifted and slunk from the jungle, making a living wall between land and sea. The locals crawled from the bush, twisting, baring their throats to Kit. They crowded onto the sand, hissing, and each holding a silver fish in their claws.

One of them tossed his at her. Kit ducked the slippery missile and it fell to the sand, bleeding, still flopping sadly. She sidestepped and scanned the beach, the brush lining it, for any path of escape. Another fish landed near the first and another. The lizards danced past her, dropping silver bodies, and as they swept by, each one twisted their neck to bare a scaly yellow throat.

"Stop it!" Kit screamed, but she could still hear Pikau's voice behind her, chanting, matching his speech to the rhythm of clawed feet, scaled tails, and the flopping of fish in the sand. "I'm not my mother."

She'd meant to shout again. If she refused, it would prove something, maybe, but her thoughts spun. The smell of blood tickled her nostrils. Had her mother really joined them in this superstition, this insanity over an outdated belief? They'd killed a lot of fish to make their point. How long would they keep at this before giving up?

What would it hurt to just…

The fish were already dead. They might flop out a few more seconds of breath, but the blood foretold their end clearly enough. All this life wasted, and if she still refused, would they keep killing? Wouldn't it make more sense to end it quickly?

Her belly clenched, suggested she reconsider. If she threw it up, would they still accept it? The damn fish were going to die anyway. The hissing pounded in her temples, as if the whole lizard horde spoke from inside her head. She pressed her paws against her ears and yowled.

Look, kitten. Understand.

Kit dropped to a crouch and snarled. The lizard tide receded, still thrashing and tossing fish at her. Pikau's voice lifted higher, screeched words she couldn't understand. She inhaled, reached for the nearest silvery corpse and pressed her eyes tight before lifting it, dragging the smell of death nearer to her lips.

Just do it fast, Kit. Don't chew. The fish felt slick in her paws, slightly sticky and squishier than she'd expected. It smelled terrible. She forced herself not to peek, to lift it to her tongue without cracking her eyelids. A metallic taste filled her mouth. She gagged, forced her jaws closed without breathing. She could do this. To keep them from killing more she could.

Something cracked hard against the back of her head. Her body plunged forward, falling onto soft sand that flopped and stank and scratched at her face. Darkness rushed in, filling her head with hissing and the beating of far off drums. Blood, blood. They chanted the volcano's request while the taste of it, the sharp metal of death swept down into Kit's belly.

***

Her mother's voice in the darkness. "Kitten, why are you crying?"

"It tastes bad, Momma. I don't want to take it."

"Shh, Kitten." Calico arms swept her into a hug. They rocked together, safe, warm… together. "It only tastes bad if you linger. Swallow it quickly."

"I don't like it." She pressed her face into her mother's fur. "I don't want to take medicine. I'm not sick."

"It's not for that, Kitten. The taurine keeps us from giving in to our instincts. It makes us stronger."

"How?" She sniffled, risked peeking at the white capsule in her mother's palm. "How can a pill do that?"

"It's magic." The humor in her mother's voice softened the lie.

"You don't believe in magic."

"Science then."

"It tastes awful."

"Swallow it quickly, and you won't taste it."

"Uh-uh."

"Swallow it."

Swallow it. Swallow.

Kit came to choking. Her mouth still tasted of blood, but she couldn't have said if she'd eaten the stupid fish or not. Her eyes blinked, adjusted to the dark surroundings. The aroma of mold and dust filled the space—not her mother's house, nor the beach or any place she'd visited in Ternate.

"Hello?" She pushed herself into a squat with shaky arms. Hard floor beneath her pads—she wasn't outdoors. "Hey! Where am I?"

The darkness held its tongue. Kit blinked away the fog in her head, and the black around her shifted to a pattern of lighter shadows. A square in the corner might be a chair. A stripe of paler wall made a rectangular line around the door.

She crept toward it, fished with one paw for a handle and found a cool knob to pull herself up. It refused to turn when she tried it, however. Locked in. She'd been shut away in the dark, and Kit could think of no *good* reason for that.

She ran her tongue around the inside of her mouth but only managed to stir the evil taste into renewed vigor. She needed a drink of water, a taurine pill, or a decent meal to wash the blood away. Not that she could ever wipe out the sin of it, or the memory.

Her paw twisted at the knob uselessly. She leaned her head against the wood and heard soft conversation beyond it.

"This is not what you said at all." Jake Marshal spoke so quietly, she barely recognized his voice. "You lied to me."

"We have no more time." That sound, the nasty hissing, Kit knew immediately. Pikau and Jake argued nearby, maybe not right outside, but close. "The volcano will not wait for you to play gentle with her."

"She has to choose. You promised."

"And she has."

"What?"

"She has eaten, Jake. It's over."

The curse word echoed much louder than the conversation, and it was followed by the hissing of Pikau, the soft tread of steps that meant to be sneaky. Kit leaped to the wall farthest from the door and crouched deep in the tiny room's darkest shadow. When the doorknob rattled, she let out a hiss of her own, let the hairs on her body all stand at attention.

She has eaten.

Would it be Pikau or Jake Marshal who opened the door? Her eyes widened, relaxed to the low light and fixed on the exit. The knob turned freely the next time. The slim line around the door widened.

It's over.

A rumble built in her chest, reverberated to the far corners of the room before Jake's flat head poked around the edge of the door. "Kitten?"

Look, Kitten. See.

"Liar." She spat the word and tensed to spring.

"No." He eased in and closed the door in the same motion, blocking her path and somehow stalling her pounce with that single, sad word. "No, Kitten. I never lied."

"You're part of it. You kept me here for him."

"I did what must be done."

"Rubbish." Her claws extended. She raked them across the floorboards, let him hear the rage she held in check. "You're not a lizard. You don't even belong here."

"What happens in this town affects us all. You should feel that by now. This place is the center of the world."

Something near her belly twisted, tugged at her from the inside. Her stomach grumbled, sounding like Gamalama. "What happens now? Will they kill me? Keep me in prison forever?"

"I've sent for your boat." Jake shrugged. "I honestly thought you wouldn't do it."

"I'm supposed to believe that?"

"It doesn't matter what you believe, Kitten. I will do whatever you ask of me."

"I definitely don't believe *that*." She scooted forward and met his gaze, searching for the lie behind his flashing. "Why would you?"

"Because you are She Who Eats." Jake Marshal stared at her. "Because I didn't keep you here, Kitten. *You* chose *to eat*."

She curled her lip up, showed him fangs that may still have had blood on them. "You'll do anything I ask?"

"Yes." Jake's laugh held only a whisper of humor. His voice was sad, filled with regret, but also resignation. His eyes never left her, and his tail swished lazily from side to side.

"What if I asked you to let me out?" Kit held her breath, held her eyes on his, and ignored the twisting in her stomach when he gave her the answer she wanted.

"Try me."

***

She meant to run all the way to the docks. She meant to test Jake's story, to see if there truly was a tiger captain waiting to take her back to Sofifi. To sanity and civilization. As soon as he opened the door for her, Kit bolted. She flew down a narrow hall and burst into an alley right in the middle of town fully intent on making her escape from them all.

She even took a half dozen steps down the slope. Kit ran in that direction far enough to see the boat, to see that he hadn't lied about it. Jake Marshal was loyal to a fault. The black and orange captain waited at his wheel, his vessel rocked on a sparkling sea, and the scent of the jungle washed down the slope of Gamalama.

Kit heard the mountain grumble, but she felt it through the toes of her rear paws. She felt the volcano's hunger in her claws and whiskers. In the way the whole world seemed to vibrate. When she turned her back on the sea, Jake waited behind her. His eyes narrowed, but all he said was, "Kitten?"

She Who Eats growled low in her throat, dug her claws in, and raced past him, upward, toward the jungle and the angry mountain beyond. She ran without thinking, without knowing where she went, and when she left the road, the fronds and vines moved aside for her. Vaguely, she sensed him following. In the back of her mind, she knew Jake would come, would be with her wherever she went now.

But she'd still have done it, even without him huffing in her wake.

Spices filled her head, and in the distance, she caught the sound of drumming, the brattle of voices raised in chant. Her path twisted and looped but led her ever upward, nearer and nearer until the beating matched her racing heart. The jungle opened upon a scene straight from one of her mother's old magazines.

The lizards danced beside a crater filled with water. The peak of Gamalama made a shadowy backdrop for the scene, and a thin line of smoke rose from the top, lifting to touch a sky studded with stars. The drumming of clawed feet against stone continued. The local's voices rose and fell with it. In their center, Pikau howled and raised his arms to the volcano in supplication.

She Who Eats stalked forward. She moved toward the crater lake, and the lizards turned black eyes in her direction. She rumbled like Gamalama, deep in her throat, and their necks twisted, their yellow throats flashed.

Not just fish. Jake had told her that, too, but she hadn't understood him. *Not that.*

Understand, Kitten.

She faltered for a breath, heard the priest's words in her mother's voice.

Wouldn't any of us go willingly to our deaths to keep the rest from harm?

Ternate held the hunger of the world at bay. Ternate, the center of the world.

Kitten.

She Who Eats watched the bared throats dancing past. She heard the beating of the blood in their veins. She smelled it on the wind. A boat waited for her below. She could still take it, turn her back and flee. No one would stop her now. No one would oppose She Who Eats.

She has to choose.

Jake stood at the jungle's edge, eyes flashing and white

hat clutched in his paws. When she died, he would march to the top of Gamalama and leap to his death. Until then, Jake Marshal and all of Ternate belonged to her. Until then, she was She Who Eats.

Let him watch and see.

Kit turned to the dancing throng and let the rumbling loose. Her growl shook the jungle fronds. Her claws raked at the soil and her volcano answered from its belly too. The world shook. The lizards bared their throats and danced. She Who Eats chose one, plucked a lizard from the crowd, and ate so that no one else would ever have to.

THE WHITE WORLD

Dark End

ANTARCTICA

"You're going to die if you keep this up, Estela."

The lynx ignored the voice and hunkered down against the snow bank. She had a pair of binoculars pressed tight to her face, which had the benefit of keeping the freezing wind out of her eyes. Even with her fur and several layers of clothes, she began to feel the Antarctic chill prickling over her skin.

"You don't need to be out here. Surely someone else can do this... this..."

"Patrol," she muttered into the scarf which wound twice around her head. Her teeth chattered a bit as she did. That wasn't a good sign, but she ignored it.

"Patrol? In Antarctica? What, are the penguins going to pick up stones and chuck them at you?"

Estela sighed and scanned the horizon again. Somewhere out here a weather station had stopped functioning and whoever had installed it had failed to record its precise location. "Stuff breaks," she said, her voice clipped. "Someone needs to fix it."

Laughter sounded in her ears. "And you thought you ought to do that, instead of some polar bear or walrus or even some stone-lobbing, barbarian penguin who might actually be suited for the weather. Why?"

"I like being alone," Estela answered. The lynx took a shuddering breath. Too quick. It filled her lungs with frigid air.

"You aren't alone, Estela. I'm here."

"You aren't real."

Another laugh, louder. "Oh, I'm as real as you."

"You aren't."

"Prove it!"

Estela couldn't keep the growl out of her voice. Sinews sprang into action, pushing her from the ground and into a standing position in an instant. She rounded on the other lynx. "Look at yourself, Hugo. You're wearing, what, swim trunks and fur? In the middle of Antarctica? You should have frostbite. You should have hypothermia. You should be dying with no hope of recovery instead of… instead of…"

He lifted an eyebrow. "Dying instead of dead, you mean?"

The wind stung her eyes. Thank God she'd long ago gotten past tearing up every time she saw this mirage of him. "Go away," she stammered as her teeth chattered again.

Hugo's short tail batted a bit at the snow where he sat a half-step away. Little wispy drifts kept trying to blow over him but faded through his noncorporeal body. "Wish I could. But I'm a product of your imagination. So I can't go away until you really want me to." He watched as Estela shivered once. "You're going to die out here, Estela, and I wish you wouldn't. Come on. Let's head back to the station."

She felt a shiver run along her spine and a sudden urge to curl up and sleep, and knew from safety training it was time to leave. She hopped on the waiting snowmobile and drove quickly back to base, with the hallucination following her the whole way.

***

Antarctic Station Zeta-3 was a series of industrial buildings connected by a spider's web of underground tunnels, all kept at a habitable temperature and humidity. The natives found it uncomfortable to be in for too long, but tourists, especially artists, loved the exotic environs and visited during the summer months, when travel in and out was easiest. By far the most common inhabitants of Zeta-3 were scientists, engineers, and explorers like Estela, coming from far-off countries to investigate the last Terran frontier.

Estela, like the other foreigners, had to make use of a locker room adjoining the entrance to peel off the many layers of warming clothes. Her fur was meant for the scrublands and rocky hills of the Iberian Peninsula, not this.

All the while she undressed and then redressed in indoor clothes, her hands shook. And here Hugo was not around to comfort her. Pain in the ass that he was, she'd much rather have him around than not.

A shiver ran down her spine and a yawn fought its way down her throat. She shook her head hard to keep herself from getting too lethargic. She *should* go see a doctor. At the very least a nurse. But she knew what they would say: rest, indoors.

Another shiver ran along her spine, one which had nothing to do with the cold outside. Already she could feel the anxiety creeping into her chest at the thought of spending time inside.

No, she did not want to see a doctor. She did not want to see anyone at all, except maybe Igor. He was the one friend she had managed to make at the station. The lynx shook herself once, shut her locker, and walked to the cafeteria.

"Ah, if it isn't our Portuguese beauty," cracked the polar bear behind the pans. "How are the sensors in the trenches of the western front? Do they still work?"

"Yes, Igor, they still work."

"Good, good." Igor grinned. He was technically only the cook, but doubled as an unofficial morale officer in the barren arctic wastes. He made it a point to know everyone at the station and to know how to lift their spirits. "We have ham casserole today. Best ham you ever tasted in Antarctica, I promise you. I smoked it myself."

Estela rolled her eyes, but otherwise humored the bear as he pushed a helping of casserole and beans with a slice of cornbread onto her plate. It was American Night at the cafeteria as it was so many nights. It would probably be Chinese night tomorrow. There might be a Portuguese night in a month or two: there just weren't that many of her nationality around. Igor constantly pestered her for recipes nonetheless, promising that he would make it special just for her.

When she went to lift the plate, it slipped from her fingers. The plate shattered on the concrete floor and bits of food flew off in all directions. "Damn it," she said numbly, having to force the words out.

"Are you okay? Is everyone okay?" The big bear rounded his little stand with surprising agility for his size and made sure there was no shards embedded in any of the nearby diners, before turning to the lynx. "Estela?"

"I'm sorry," she said, knowing she couldn't hide the truth— not all of it anyway. She held out one shaky hand. "I stayed out a bit too long and got cold. You got something that will warm me up, and fast?"

Igor scurried back into the kitchen. Everyone else got back to work, but he focused his attention completely on her. The bear came out a minute later with a bowl of chili, which had a sealed top to keep it from spilling. He pressed it against her shaking paws and she relished in the heat that seeped from the bowl and into her fingers. "I'll take it to my room," Estela said, and Igor tucked a spoon and napkins into her jacket pocket. He kept asking over and over if she was all right. The lynx wasn't sure if she felt smothered or pampered; she decided that if nothing else, she was glad for the contact, however brief, with another living, breathing person.

She was tempted for a moment to stay in the cafeteria. Igor was always full of stories, often of his own misbegotten youth, and listening to them was one of the few pleasures she had inside the station. But her hand ached and shivered and she knew she had to go.

She shuffled her way down to the residential part of the complex. This meant using an underground tunnel between the buildings, which felt old and rickety like a catacomb, although it had been built in the last ten years. When she made it back to her room, she turned the thermometer's setting up and wrapped her ice-cold hands in a blanket.

The chili was tempting. Its scent kept teasing at her nose, and a thought popped into her mind of how much Hugo would like to have some.

She quashed that thought even faster than the one about visiting the doctor. Anxiety pricked at her heart and she tried to focus as much as she could on feeling better.

It took nearly thirty minutes of shivering before her hands warmed up enough. Once they had, her position, sprawled out on the bed, was too comfortable. Her form had curled up like that of a kitten. She found she didn't want to move and slept right there.

When she came to in the morning, alarm blaring well before sunrise, one of the first things she did was dump the now cold chili into the garbage. She made a note to tell Igor it had been great.

Then, with her stomach growling, the lynx wandered out for breakfast.

***

Estela shoved her shoulder against the long handle of the wrench. "What sort of idiot assembled this thing off-continent?" She shoved again and the wrench moved, barely. Every piece of metal had shrunk in the cold and lodged into place. She couldn't even tell what it was supposed to be as the weather-beaten exterior had lost most of its paint and markings. Supposedly it was her missing weather station from the previous day, but there was no way of knowing for sure until she got inside.

"You're getting worse," Hugo said. He was sprawled out on

the snowmobile, still clad in nothing more than a pair of swim trunks. The lynx's ears barely moved despite the howling wind.

"I am not," she grunted before throwing her weight into the wrench. It finally gave and the bolt came out a quarter turn.

"Hypothermia," he suggested.

"Hypothermia is short-term. I should have been fine after all night indoors last night." She hit her hands against her thighs to try and get some warmth back into them. In truth, she had felt a little better in the morning, with a warm cup of coffee clutched in both hands and Igor's stories in her ears. No one else seemed to appreciate them like she did.

"Cold exhaustion, then."

"Not a thing." She kept twisting the wrench until the last bolt popped out and fell onto the ground. But when she gripped the metal panel that was covering the device's innards, she found it had lodged in place. "Oh. Come. On." Grunts filled the air as she jerked and twisted, but the panel failed to budge.

"Exhaustion then. Plain old exhaustion. The body starts failing in magnificent ways under extreme stress."

Estela's shoulders sagged. A look over her shoulder confirmed the illusory lynx was still sprawled out on the snowmobile. He looked so carefree and relaxed. But his eyes were on her. They were always on her. "Fine. Exhaustion. Are you satisfied now?"

Hugo sat up on the edge of the snowmobile, one leg dangling off like he was dipping a toe into a warm pool. "I'd be happier if you went back and rested up for a few days," he said in an echo of her own thoughts from yesterday. "Tell someone else they need to come look at all the gizmos they have out here."

"No, I'll do it." She tried to get a different angle. The panel had a big lip around the edge and she tried shoving it with her shoulder again.

Hugo appeared suddenly on top of the device, staring down at her, his little tail twitching. "Why does it have to be you?"

"Because of you!" Estela screamed suddenly. She picked up the wrench and threw it at Hugo. It passed through the hallucination without ever noticing it was there and lodged itself in a snowdrift behind him. "Oh damn it," she said and hurried to dig it out.

Hugo walked behind her. He had both hands on his neck, rubbing it as if ashamed. "What did I do, Estela? Please, tell me."

"You're back there," she said, pointing with the recovered wrench back to the station.

"I'm here too," the male lynx said, confused. "I mean, I'm only a figment of your imagination, but I'm here."

"Yeah," Estela said glumly. "But out here at least all you do is talk." She got back to the device and looked at the wrench in her hand. Figuring most of it was doomed for the scrapheap (or abandonment) she smacked the wrench into the lip of the panel. It popped free and with a triumphant whoop, she gripped the edges and tore it back. As she did she heard fabric tearing.

"Aw, damn it. I liked those gloves…" The words trailed out of her mouth and into the icy winds.

"Estela, what is it?"

The edge of the panel had torn a neat gash right through the glove and along her hand. Bright red blood trickled out. "I don't even feel it."

Looking alarmed, the male lynx said hurriedly, "Estela, back to the station. Now!"

For once, she didn't argue.

***

The door to Estela's room at Zeta-3 banged loudly. It roused the lynx from her nap. "What? Who?"

"It is me, Igor," came the voice through the door. "I have dinner for you."

"Oh, thanks, but I'll just come pick it up in a bit," she said a little loudly, to make herself heard around the thick door.

"Ah, but cafeteria is already closed," he said in more stilted English than normal. He was speaking faster and more of his Russian accent slipped through.

Estela rubbed her eyes (momentarily surprised by the bandages around one hand until she remembered why they were there) and checked the clock. Eleven PM. Already? How long had she been out? She parsed together the recent events. She had come back to the station, seen the doctor, been told to take a week off, no questions, conjured up some imaginary sleep troubles, and conked out on too many drugs back at her room.

Slowly, she stood, stretched, flexed her claws once or twice, then opened the door.

Igor burst in, his rotund form filling up most of the extra space in the room. In his outstretched hands he held a tray: spiced roast chicken, roast vegetables, and an extra large slice of some kind of cake, thankfully not roasted. It wasn't quite Chinese night, although she was pretty sure there was bok choy in the vegetables. "I did not see you at dinner and after hearing about your injury today, I worry."

Estela sat back in bed, tray in her lap, and started cutting into the chicken hungrily. At least her hands were steady now, even if her cut palm started aching every time it moved. That was better than feeling nothing at all, though.

"Are you all right?"

"You keep asking me that, Igor. The answer's not going to change much," she said in between bites. "I just want to get back to work."

"The doctor said—"

"I am aware of what the doctor said!" Estela yelled and immediately regretted it. She didn't look up at him. She imagined the bear would be hurt, and he was the only friend she had here. She didn't want to see that. She didn't want to lose that friendship.

Igor sniffed the air once and then leaned over to take a peek into the trashcan. "It is good I bring you dinner tonight.

It looks like you did not have much last night."

Estela mentally hit herself: the chili was still in there. "I've had a rough few days."

The bear gave a slow nod. In the kitchen he wore an over-sized sky blue apron over pristine white shirt and pants. Now he was in sedate blacks and browns that matched his fur better. Estela couldn't remember ever having him wearing clothes like that before. "It is good to talk while you eat, so here, I will talk and you can listen. I tell story of my youth, funny story."

Estela perked up. No matter how bad she felt, Igor's stories were always welcome. She kept shoveling food in as she listened. She was famished and silently thanked Igor from the deepest part of her heart for thinking to bring her food.

"So I was a soldier many years ago. I am poor. I cannot bribe my way to a good position, so they put me in a fort on the edge of some starving town. And all I do for months is guard duty. You ever seen someone on guard duty? They shove a gun in your arms and draw a little square around you. They tell you to watch. They tell you no one is allowed in your square. Anyone tries to get in your square, you shoot them.

"One day this general is visiting the base. He is—how would you say it? The British have such good words for this—mangy flea-bitten cur. He is a little drunk and tries to taunt the guards. He gets a bit too close to my square, so I put a hole through the hat he was wearing. It was a very nice hat. Was not so nice after that."

Estela nearly choked as she chewed on some bok choy.

"Ah, but that is not best part of the story. You see, we were bored in the evenings. It wasn't our shift anymore. No reason to stay, and no reason to leave the fort. So we do what any good youngsters do: we make booze."

"Vodka?" she asked between bites.

"Feh." Igor flicked a hand dismissively. "Is only true vodka if it is made from potatoes. We didn't have any. We used rice. We had always too much rice.

"Anyway, there were six of us, and five of us every night

would go down and work the still and get drunk. Good way to spend an evening. Except for Milos. Little weasel. He would never come join us. He would wander off in the evenings and when he came back late at night, he had the scent of blood around him." He paused his story for just a moment to gesture at Estela's cut hand and then, as if embarrassed, he quickly continued with his story. "I start to get worried.

"This goes on for week after week. And week after week I am feeling worse and worse, and worrying more and more. Eventually I follow him. He is going up on the walls, looking down at the people outside. They are huddled, tired, cold, dying. Every time he sees one of them die, he pulls out a little knife and adds a little cut to his shoulder."

Unchewed pieces of chicken dangled from Estela's lips. "What the hell did he do that for?"

Igor frowned and chewed his lip a moment. "He grew up idolizing soldiers. He thought he was supposed to be a protector. He felt responsible. Each soul lost was one mark against him. He was keeping track of his failures."

"I thought you said this was a funny story."

"Ah, it does get better! You see, I saw him doing this and could not let it go on. I pick him up by the scruff. (Easy to do: he was very little weasel.) I carry him kicking and screaming and yowling all the way to the still, and then I dunk his head in the barrel of booze until he drinks. Then I pull out a cup and drink. Then I shove a cup in his hand and he drinks. Then we both drink and drink and drink and drink.

"Next morning, there is a—how do you say—commotion on the base. There is a terrible noise and even worse smell. They find us up on the walls of the fort. We are naked as the day we are born, dancing jigs with a bottle of booze in each hand, laughing so hard it can be heard across town, and every now and then seeing how far we can vomit over the edge. Ah, I have never been so drunk in my life. And I have never been yelled at so much before either. It hurt a lot. I was very hung over by that time. But it was worth it. Milos never went on the walls to watch the people die again."

Estela bit into a few more vegetables, swallowed, and spoke. "It was that easy to change him, huh?"

"He could not see anything but the misery. And he went away every night to bathe in it and feel it right against his bones. I had to show him there was still laughter in the world. And once I did he had no need to go away anymore."

Estela nodded.

Igor leaned forward, resting his hands on his knees. "So why do you go away?"

"Huh?" Estela looked up quizzically from her bite of cake.

"You had a good career, a promising life, and you turn it all down to come out here fixing junk in the last frontier. Why? You don't even like it here. I've heard you say so yourself, and the place you came from is so beautiful." He gestured to a picture on the nightstand.

It was a picture of her at the beach back home.

The beach…

She slammed the picture down and out of sight with such ferocity that Igor jerked backward and nearly hit his head against the far wall of her room.

"I am sorry," he said. "I heard about your cut, and I thought about Milos…" His voice grew weaker. The big bear stood suddenly. "I made a mistake. I will leave."

"No." Estela was on her feet almost as fast as he was. She had to be careful with the tray in her hands, though. "Please, I'd like you to stay." She shifted from foot to foot uneasily. "And thank you…for thinking of me." She offered an uncertain smile.

It was the bear's turn to feel embarrassed. "It was nothing. I would do it for anyone."

"Would you?"

The bear coughed a little. "The pretty ones at least."

Estela was flattered that he thought she was pretty. But her thoughts drifted back to the picture of the beach, and her smile faltered.

Igor went from embarrassed to mortified. "That was crude of me, wasn't it? I should go."

"No, no, it's not that. It's…nothing. Igor, please." She gestured to the chair he had been using. "At least one more story before you go. I could use a friend."

"A friend, yes," the bear said with an edge of uncertainty in his voice. After teetering for a minute, the bear finally relented, and with a laugh, began another story.

***

Estela woke up in the morning and rolled over in her little bed, arm reaching out to curl around…

Nothing.

Her eyes snapped open. Her hand was trying to hold onto a bundle of air. There was nothing in bed with her but the sheets and the pillow. As it had always been for the last few years.

She bit back the wave of sickness inside her and focused on getting ready for the day. She didn't have to go out—the forecast called for terrible conditions. So the lynx put on something light and went out for a morning jog. "Out" in this case just meant around the indoor gym, but it was good, got her blood flowing, made her forgetful.

By the time she had made it to the cafeteria, she had started to smile. A wet towel wound around her neck and pushed cold moisture into her fur, cooling her down quickly. Igor was there, and he smiled as she came up and held out the tray from the previous night. "Breakfast?" he offered.

"Coffee first. Always coffee first."

Of course, the bear already knew that. Before she had finished speaking, he was turned to the huge espresso machine beside him, imported at great expense but with great praise as it replaced the terrible drip coffee. "What will it be?"

"One latte and one ristretto with a touch of whipped cream on top."

"Two drinks this morning?" the bear shrugged as he started

grinding the beans. "Are you sure you need so much?"

"Oh, it's not for me. The ristretto is for..." And it hit her again. "For Hugo," she said under her breath. She doubled over, the loss of him hitting her right in her chest. It felt like a knife had been shoved under her sternum, twisting about, tearing her heart to ribbons.

"Estela!" Igor shouted. "What's wrong?" Somehow he was already around the counter and holding her shoulders.

The lynx ignored him.

Emotions tore inside her. Not only the feeling of loss, but the dread of losing him again and the terror at realizing that she was trapped inside for days.

She twisted out of the bear's grip and ran. She focused herself purely on the running, feeling the pain of loss fading again. There was only so much room she could run inside the compound, and she knew the feelings would follow her. They always did. She had to get out.

Igor was behind her somewhere, shouting. But he was no match for her in speed.

Estela had left all her warm clothes back in her room, but they always kept emergency warm wear by the exits. The lynx grabbed a puffy jacket and was still threading her arms into it as she burst into the storm. The cold hit her across the face and sunk deep into her bones. The jacket may have been warm, but she had almost nothing on underneath it. Her legs immediately began to burn from the combination of being pushed too hard and the sudden chill.

"Don't." It was Hugo. He was standing in front of her. As she kept going, his illusory form hovered in front of her, just out of arms reach. "Estela, please, you'll die."

"I'll die if I stay," she huffed, her teeth already chattering. She was bent forward against the wind, fighting for each step. The storm was fierce. She was probably no more than a mile from the station, but she couldn't see it in the swirling snow.

"Estela, be reasonable!"

"I am being reasonable."

"You're hurting yourself being out here."

"It hurts to be anywhere," she shouted over the wind. Crazy woman, she thought to herself, screaming at a mirage at the bottom of the world. "And all because of you."

The male lynx looked down, distressed. "I didn't mean to hurt you."

Estela, enraged, wound up for a punch. "You should have thought of that before you died, you asshole." She swung at him, her fist sailing straight through.

Momentum carried her forward, over the edge of an embankment, and she tumbled down a massive snowdrift. End over end she rolled through the powder, until she came at last to a stop at the bottom, aching everywhere, shivering. Unable to move.

"You've got to get up," Hugo said morosely.

"I can't." She tried and tried, but the pain was too much. The cold had found its way deep inside. She curled up inside the coat, trying to conserve the tiny amount of warmth that she did have.

"You have to."

"I said I can't!"

"Estela!"

"Shut up, Hugo!"

He looked down at her. "That wasn't me, love."

The female lynx looked around.

"Estela!" came the call again.

"Down here," she tried to say, but her voice was weak and the wind was howling.

It didn't matter. Igor found her, his head popping up over the ridge and then his whole form lumbering down afterwards. He did not listen to the words she tried to say. He had emergency gear with him, wrapping her up in a blanket and pressing a warm fluid to her lips, which she drank greedily. He seemed so well prepared. Had she already been gone so long he had time to double back for gear? Was the cold messing with her that much?

Igor pulled her body in against his. His fur was thick and warm. She found herself pressing instinctively into it, feeling like a cub nestling into its mother.

"I'm so sorry," the bear said. "I do not know what it was. I did not realize I would make you run out here in the cold like this. I am such an idiot." He said more words into a phone. She couldn't make them out, but she thought he was calling off a search party.

"It wasn't you," Estela managed to say after warming up a moment more. "It was Hugo." She looked around. She saw him kneeling down beside the bear. He was still worried, but less so now that Igor had found her.

"Who is…Hugo?"

"My husband."

"Ah, I did not realize you were… with someone. I would not have… You know."

She shook her head and pressed in against him a moment more. Lucky bear, she thought, didn't need all this stupid gear. He belonged out here. She didn't. "Can I be the one to tell you the story this time?" she asked, quietly.

Igor nodded so quickly his whole body shook around her.

"It was a few years ago. Hugo and I were at the beach in Praia da Rocha. I had a blanket and some stupid book I was reading, and he wanted to go play in the water. There were a bunch of kids out there splashing in the shallows, and he loved to play with them. He was a good sport. He let them push him over and was never mean."

Igor held her. He could probably barely hear her story, but his ears were turned towards her nonetheless. Hugo knelt beside him, still in those stupid paisley-print swim shorts he had worn that day.

"It got late, and I… I just wanted to go home. I had finished my book and had a little headache. I asked him to come with, but he wanted to chat with some friends on the beach. He told me he'd catch up to me back at the house; it was only a few blocks away. So I went. I just left him there. My headache grew worse so I went to bed. I woke up the following morning and he hadn't returned. That's when I got the call. His body had been found: there'd been a strong riptide, and he'd been pulled out to sea and drowned."

She shivered, but not because she was cold. "Hugo always loved that ristretto with a hit of whipped cream. I'd make one for him every day right at a quarter after five, so it would be finishing up right as he walked in the door. I made one that day. I'd forgotten. Between morning and afternoon, I'd forgotten that he'd died. And when he didn't come home, and I remembered why, it hurt all over again."

Igor's expression did not change, but Hugo's got progressively worse. He looked ready to cry.

"I made that damn ristretto every weekday for five months! I kept forgetting he was supposed to be dead. And every time I remembered it hurt just like it did the first time. I'd wake up in the morning and think for ten minutes that the reason why he wasn't in bed with me was that he'd gotten up early and started making breakfast. His office buddies would call from time to time, to check in on me, and I would ask them every time if he was staying late. They had to remind me that he was gone."

It hurt to cry when it was so cold out. Her nose was running too, and the icy feeling was clawing inside her nostrils. Hugo was crying and sniffling right along with her.

"So I went away," she said. "I started leaving behind everything I could, everything that would remind me of the way things were when he was alive. And I didn't stop until I was at the end of the world out here, when I could finally remember he was gone and it stopped hurting. That's why I work such long hours. Because even at the station, I start to forget, but out here I don't. I can't. He doesn't stop reminding me."

Igor gave a start. "What?"

Estela sighed. "I... I see him. Right there, beside you." She gestured.

Igor's head spun around. "You mean like a ghost?"

"I mean like a hallucination. I'm crazy, Igor. I'm sick. I have been for a long time."

"I could have told you that just by you coming out here."
His big eyes swung from Estela to the spot she had pointed
to. "They let you come out here, as…" He stumbled over the
words, as if trying not to say the one word they both knew he
should: "crazy." "As sick as you are?"

Estela shrugged. She was warming up now at least. Or the
cold wasn't affecting her as badly. "They were desperate for
competent techs, and I was deemed 'not a danger to others,' so
they didn't care. Besides, out here, it's better. He talks to me.
He doesn't let me forget. He's too… wrong, still wearing swim
trunks even though it's freezing out here."

Igor's brow furrowed. And he kept looking back and forth
between Estela and the spot she had gestured too, looking
straight through Hugo on the way. "So, he is like a good ghost
then?"

"What?"

"He says helpful things?"

She nodded and a small smile came to Hugo's face as she
did. "He keeps me from staying out here too long."

"Then you are not so sick. But, all being same, we should
get you back inside. You will freeze out here. Even I will freeze
out here given enough time."

"No!" Estela said, a rising panic filling her. "No, please, it
will hurt again."

"Hmph, and what does your ghost say?"

She didn't look at Hugo. "What?"

"You said he says helpful things. I bet he is telling you to
go with me, eh?"

She sighed and rolled her eyes, looking for the lynx. He
was standing at Igor's side and whispering, although it wasn't as
though Igor would hear. "Do it."

"He's not," Estela said.

"He did not turn bad ghost on you, did he? What is he
saying?"

"He's saying to do it."

"Do what?"

Estela shrugged.

Hugo hit himself on the forehead. "Kiss him, you fool!"

Estela stared dumbly at the phantom lynx. "What?"

"Kiss him." Hugo was practically stomping at the ground. "Do you honestly think he has done these things, checked in on you, come out into this blazing snowstorm, because that's who he is? He likes you. He might even love you. And you've been too blinded worrying about me to notice. So kiss him and be done with it."

Estela looked back at the bear. Part of her knew Hugo was right. He was, as he said, just a figment of her imagination, speaking the truth she could not admit to herself otherwise. But another part of her still doubted and was still afraid of forgetting it all again. Before the fear could take hold of her once again, she lunged forward, muzzle almost smashing into Igor's, and she kissed him as fiercely as she dared. Despite the wind snapping around her head and blowing her fur every which way, she felt warmer than she had in a long time.

Igor pulled back, a bit shocked. "A very good ghost," he muttered.

Estela looked around for Hugo. But he had disappeared, or almost so. She caught the faint glimpse of his smile, lingering in the air, before it too was swept away. "He's gone."

"He did his job, I think. Come on." He hefted her body easily in his hands and began the trek back towards the compound. "I have many more stories to tell you, and they are much funnier than nearly shooting commanding officer."

Estela rested her head on his chest and for the first time in many, many years, looked forward to tomorrow.

WATERLOGGED

Madison Keller

PORTLAND, USA

Sam slapped her long, flat tail on the docks watching the otter police divers swim the corpse to shore. As they drew close, the spotlights illuminated light-brown fur, a stocky body, webbed feet, and a flat tail like her own. A beaver. Dead in the Willamette River.

A bubblegum bubble snapped in her ear, signifying her partner, Parker Ringschein, had joined her. With black facial masks and striped tails, his kind had historically been marked as bandits. Innate tricksters. Parker had decided to become a cop against everyone's expectations. A real rebel.

"Stop that stupid popping," Sam said without taking her eyes off the still form in the water. "Can't you have a little respect for the dead?"

Parker snorted in disgust, and a moment later a blob of gum splashed into the river. "Nicotine gum. Promised the wife I'd quit smoking."

Sam grinned and patted his shoulder. "About time."

The otters reached the docks and hauled the corpse onto the tarp. The dead beaver was male, young, possibly early twenties, and quite handsome. Tall for a beaver. He had a long muzzle, light-brown velvety fur, and slightly darker underfur. His tattered clothing was of the latest cuts and styles. His flat tail was pierced in multiple places by diamond studs.

Sam pulled on gloves and knelt beside the corpse, ignoring the water that soaked into her pant legs. "I'd say he's been in the water for at least two days. Judging from the lack of wounds on the body, I'm pretty certain he drowned."

Parker blinked. "Drowned? A beaver? That's crazy."

Sam shrugged. "I agree, but we'll have to wait for the coroner's report to be sure. Now, let's see if we can figure out who our John Doe Beaver here is."

Sam patted the victim's pockets. Sadly, she came up empty. The wallet was gone, most likely lost to the river's current.

Parker, being Parker, went right for the beaver's gold watch. "Fancy," he said as he pulled it off. "Expensive, too. So sad about the water damage." Parker flipped the watch over and held it up before slipping it into an evidence bag.

"His, I wonder, or someone else's?" Sam said, distracted. She ran her webbed paws through the fur on the dead beaver's arm. His underfur was thinner than she had expected it to be. Anyone but another beaver probably wouldn't notice the difference.

"Guess it's up to us to find out." Parker grinned. "We've made do with less."

"True." Sam rubbed the cuff of the shirt. Expensive material, quick-dry like her own suit but of much higher quality. "No wallet, but this wasn't a mugging gone south. If it was they would have taken the watch and the diamond studs before dumping him in the Willamette."

Parker nodded. "Rich mammal like this, someone will have noticed him gone. Missing Persons is our best bet to find out his name."

***

Parker turned out to be right. A quick search of the missing person's database from his smartphone netted them a report that had come in less than an hour before for a beaver named Dillon Dam.

From the attached photo, he was definitely their floater. To Sam's surprise, Dillon wore holey flannels and dirty jeans in the picture. His arm draped companionably around the back of a kneeling, yellow Labrador.

"He worked at Lucky Labrador as a *bartender?*" Sam read in growing disbelief. She buckled herself in the passenger seat of their unmarked police car, then pulled out her own phone and searched the Internet for the watch they'd pulled off Dillon. "That watch alone would cost three times more than he likely made in a year."

Parker shrugged and started the car, turning on the windshield wipers to catch the light mist that had started to fall. "Maybe he was a thief or drug dealer? Too early to speculate. If he's into something that got him killed, maybe his boss would know."

The coroner's van pulled away, headed for the morgue, and Parker followed it from the dock. They turned off onto the Morrison bridge and went east across the river toward the Lucky Lab.

"You ever been to the Lab?" Parker asked her as they wended their way deeper into the east side.

Sam shook her head. "No. I know it's a Portland landmark, but it's so far from the river. Plus, I heard it's a human hangout."

Parker laughed as he parked. "Humans can be alright. But yeah, if you aren't comfortable with them, the Lab is a bad choice for a night out."

Sam enjoyed the rain on her fur as they walked to the Lucky Lab half a block up, clustered with a few other small businesses. The only places open this time of night catered exclusively to nocturnals. Nocturnal licensed bars could serve alcohol later than regular bars. Most of the folks passing by were of that bent: stoats, possums, raccoons, bats, skunks, coyotes, and cats. Sam appeared to be the only aquatic this far from the river, which made Dillon's employment here even more puzzling.

To her relief there weren't any humans outside. The doorman turned out to be the yellow Lab from the Missing Persons photo.

"ID?" the Labrador barked, holding out a paw.

"Not here to drink. I'm Detective Digger. This is my partner Detective Ringschein." Sam flashed him her badge then gestured to the raccoon who'd ambled up behind her. "Are you Ozzy Waggeth? The one who reported Dillon missing?" Parker was the more outgoing of the two, but by unspoken agreement she took the lead on this case. Beavers needed to watch out for each other.

The dog's ears drooped and his constantly wagging tail slowed. "Yes. It's... It's bad, isn't it? I thought, hoped, he'd just gone on a bender. But if you're here..." He swallowed.

Sam hated this part of her job. "I'm afraid so. Dillon's body was recovered from the river earlier this evening."

Ozzy's tail curled between his legs. "Oh, Dillon," he whined, hugging his arms to himself. As his paws ran over his fur they revealed shallow scratches on his wrists and arms.

"We'll need to speak to the manager of the bar." Sam shuffled uncomfortably at the dog's display of grief. "But first, can you tell us the last time you saw Dillon?"

"Night 'fore last. Saturday night. We were busy. Last I saw of him he was taking off at the end of our shifts. He was supposed to work last night, but didn't show." The dog covered his eyes with a paw. "Dillon does that sometimes, so we weren't too worried. But when he didn't show up again tonight..."

"Do you know where he might have gone when he left here Sunday morning?" Sam asked.

Parker shuffled forward and offered the dog his handkerchief.

"No, but Rick would." Ozzy blew into it loudly and shook his head, making his ears ripple.

"Rick?" Sam scribbled the name into her pad, along with her notes about the dog's story.

Ozzy's eyes narrowed and a growl escaped his lips as he

pointed inside. "The human sitting alone at the bar. Brown hair, glasses."

"A friend of Dillon's?" Sam slapped her flat tail on the ground in irritation. Why did it have to be a human? Sam looked at the human Ozzy pointed out. He slumped over the bar, his eyes glued to a phone held in front of him. A half-full pint sat by his hand. Sam judged he'd be there a while yet. Time enough to talk to the manager.

"Yeah." Ozzy moved inside and waved at another employee, a lean black cat. "Hey, watch the door for a sec. I gotta take these two to see Dave."

Ozzy led Sam and Parker through the bar, which was about half full, then barged through a door labeled "Employees Only", startling a fat, black Labrador behind the desk inside. The dog looked up from his computer with a guilty expression. Before he slapped the laptop closed Sam caught a glimpse of porn playing on the screen. Sam rolled her eyes.

"Dave," Ozzy barked. "Dillon's dead! Murdered!"

"What?" Dave looked with alarm at the two detectives.

"Now wait, I never said that." Sam put her paws on her hips and slapped her tail.

Ozzy shot her a look like she was crazy. "You said you pulled his body out of the river. He's a beaver. What else could it be but murder?"

Sam sighed. "We suspect foul play, yes, but we haven't yet confirmed murder. It could have been an accident."

"Anything we can do to help." Dave gestured a paw at the two seats in front of his desk.

Sam waddled over and climbed up onto the large chair, sized for humans or Labradors, not for smaller beavers or raccoons. Parker hung back, stuffing a stick of gum into his mouth, his bright black eyes roving over the room. Ozzy shut the door, but remained inside listening.

"First things first, we'll need to contact Dillon's next of kin. Do you have the name and number of his emergency contact?"

Dave's chair squeaked as he spun around to reach the filing

cabinet behind his desk. After a few moments rifling around he pulled out a thin manila folder stamped with Dillon's name.

"Here you go." Dave presented it to her.

Sam flipped through it, jotting down the name and phone number of one Eric Russel, Dillon's emergency contact, into her notepad. It didn't sound like a beaver name. She also scribbled down Dillon's address, which to her surprise was on the south-east side, far from the aquatic neighborhoods along Lake Smith-Bybee and the Willamette and Columbia Rivers.

"Did Dillon have any enemies? Or a problem with any of the patrons or other bartenders?" Sam asked, handing the file back to Dave.

Dave shook his head, sending his jowls flapping. "No, no, everyone loved Dillon."

At the same time Ozzy said, "There was that one guy…"

Sam's gaze snapped back to Ozzy, who hung his head. "Tell me more," she said.

"Dillon got in a fight about six months back, with some human patron. Used to be a regular, but I never saw him again after that night," Ozzy said with a shrug.

"Either of you know what the fight was about?" Sam asked.

Ozzy shook his head. "I didn't hear the beginning of it. I only saw the end when I was called in to bounce him."

Dave answered next. "No, but I remember that now. Only black mark on Dillon's record. Gave him a talking to the next day, and he assured me it'd never happen again."

Sam considered it. If the fight was a few months ago it probably didn't have anything to do with Dillon's death. No point in chasing dead ends. "Alright, thanks. If you think of anything else that might help me give me a call." She pulled two business cards out of her wallet and laid them on the edge of Dave's desk before climbing down.

Ozzy showed them back into the bar before returning to his place at the front door. The human still sat at the bar, nursing his beer and staring at his phone.

"What'd you think about Dave and Ozzy?" Sam asked

Parker as she pulled out her phone. They'd moved over to the corner of the bar to talk privately.

"They were both genuinely upset about Dillon's death." Parker shrugged.

"I agree." Sam paused. "But I do wonder why Ozzy immediately assumed murder. I mean, it could just be an accident. Drunk beaver falls in the river. If he was too drunk to walk, he'd be too drunk to swim. It's rare, but not unheard of."

Parker frowned, twitching his whiskers. "Guess we'll have to wait for the autopsy report and the tox screen to come back."

"Yeah." Sam sighed as she plugged Eric's number into her phone. "I want to inform the emergency contact now, before we do anything else."

Parker nodded. "I'll keep an eye on this Rick fellow, make sure he doesn't scarper while you're talking."

Sam gave him a webbed thumbs-up as she put the phone to her ear, waddling toward the front door at the same time. The first ring buzzed in her ear. At the bar, Rick's phone began to jingle. Sam stopped and turned. Rick fumbled with the screen as the phone rang again. Finally, his blundering fingers found the answer button and Sam watched as he lifted the phone. A drunk "Hello?" slurred into her ear.

"Oh, you've got to be kidding me." Sam disconnected.

Rick pulled the phone back and stared at it in surprise while Sam waddled back toward him, slapping her tail angrily behind her. Parker doubled over a barstool, laughing his striped tail off. Sam shot him a nasty glance before she reached Rick.

"Rick. Eric Russel?" She poked the human's leg to get his attention.

The human set his phone down and turned on his stool, scanning the bar overtop of Sam's head. "Huh, thought I heard my name?"

"Yeah, down here!" Sam's tail struck the wooden floor again with a solid whack.

"Oh my gosh!" Rick slid off his stool and crouched in front of her. Alcohol fumes from his breath stung her nose. "Aren't you just so cute!"

"Sir, I'm a detective with the Portland City Police Department." Sam held her badge up into the human's face while she backed up a few steps. "Are you Eric Russel, Dillon Dam's emergency contact?"

"Dillon?" Rick's face screwed up and water started leaking from his eyes. Sam had to squash a shudder. Humans' fur-bald, flat faces always looked so strange to her and usually she had a hard time reading their emotions, but not tonight. Rick was clearly upset about something.

"Sir, I'm sorry to inform you that Dillon's body was recovered from the Willamette River several hours ago."

Rick fell back into the bar, landing on his butt. "Dillon... Dillon's dead?"

"Yes, I'm sorry." Inspiration struck her. If he was living with a human that would explain the odd east-side address. "Was he your roommate?"

"I-I guess." Rick swiped at his face with his sleeve.

Sam frowned. "It wasn't a trick question, Mr. Russell. Did he live with you?"

"Yes," Rick slurred through tears.

"We suspect there may be foul play involved. We'll need to search his room." Sam steeled herself and waddled forward, laying a comforting, webbed paw on Rick's knee. He was genuinely broken up over the death of his roommate.

Rick shook his head. "No, I can't let you do that."

By now Parker had come over and was watching the exchange with interest. "We can get a warrant, Rick."

Sam shot Parker an irritated glance. "Do you have any contact information for Dillon's family? They'll need to be informed as well."

"No, I don't. Dillon didn't get along with his family. That's why he moved out to Portland, to get away from them."

Now that Sam could understand. She herself had moved from Salem to escape her mother's constant harping about finding a mate and questions about when she was going to see grand-kits.

"Do you know where he was from?" Beavers as a whole were fairly rare, but Dam was a very common last name.

Rick shrugged. "He never told me, exactly. I know his sister at least was in his phone contacts 'cause he talked to her last week."

Sam jotted this down in her notebook. The phone had been on the body, but was waterlogged and the data most likely unrecoverable. They could get the records from his service provider, but it would take a few weeks. "Do you know what they talked about?"

"No, but whatever it was made Dillon very upset." Rick hiccupped and wiped his face.

"Ozzy told us that you might know where Dillon went after he left work two nights ago." Sam tapped her pencil against her pad.

Rick shook his head and a fat tear rolled down his cheek. "I—No, I don't. I came by the bar after work, like I usually do. He gave me his car keys, told me to go home without him and not to wait up – that he had an appointment after work. He never came home and I never saw him again."

Sam's whiskers twitched. "An appointment with who?"

"I don't know. He didn't tell me." Rick sniffled again. "He had an overnight bag with him, though."

The kid was stonewalling, closing up. This wasn't getting them anywhere. "We'll be by later with a warrant for Dillon's room. In the meantime, if you do think of anything else, here's my card." Sam handed him one of her business cards.

She and Parker waddled back toward the door. As they exited, Sam turned to Ozzy, slinging a thumb over her shoulder at the drunk, sobbing form of Rick under the bar. "Call him a cab."

***

Sam slept fitfully through the day, dreaming of Dillon and

water. As a consequence, she waddled into the station late that evening, yawning and nursing a cup of coffee. Parker was already at their shared desk, his dark eyes bright and whiskers twitching as his nimble paws flipped through a paper file.

"Morning! Bright eyed and bushy tailed as usual, I see." Parker giggled at his own joke.

"Did our search turn up any of Dillon's family?" Sam asked, slumping into her chair. She'd long since found the best way to get under Parker's fur was to ignore him.

"No, but the autopsy report came in," Parker said, handing her a piece of paper.

Sam held the paper inches from her muzzle, struggling to focus her tired eyes. Finally she slapped the report down on the desk in frustration and leaned back on her tail. "Cause of death: drowning. We already knew that."

Parker smirked. "You missed the important part."

"Not in the mood, just tell me." Sam sipped her coffee.

"They tested the water in his lungs. It was tap water."

Sam groaned. "So it was murder." In her heart she'd hoped it had just been an accident.

"But we do have a lead." Parker leaned over and picked up a cardboard box that had been hidden at his feet. "While I was waiting for you, I went through Dillon's personal effects. There was a receipt from the downtown branch of Voodoo Donuts. Looks like he went there shortly before his death."

"Downtown is for tourists. Locals know it's less crowded at the other branches, and the donuts are just as good, so what's the only reason a seasoned Portlander would go to Voodoo's downtown branch?" The downtown branch was the place that had started it all, and tourists flocked to Portland from across the US to visit. The original store was now a shrine, with the donuts being sold from the attached new construction. Sam had remembered when her mother came to visit her. She had insisted on going to the downtown location despite Sam's pleas because her mother wanted to say she'd visited the original.

"When someone is in from out of town…" Parker's eyes lit

up and he nodded his head for her to continue.

Sam set down her cup and swiped up the keys to their patrol car. "What do you want to bet that his important appointment was to take his out-of-town sister to Voodoo?"

Parker grinned and stood, pulling on his coat. "You sure you want to make a bet with a raccoon, Digger?"

"Only when it's a sure thing."

At the early hour of the evening it was a mixed crowd of mammals: foxes, otters, cats, rats, skunks, humans, and even foreign animals like zebras, hippos, tigers, and pandas. Cries of "cutter" followed her and Parker as they bypassed the line and pushed through the front doors. A large bison, biceps straining the seams of her security shirt, stopped them before they got three steps into the pink, boxy building.

Sam and Parker flashed their police badges. "We're here on official business, ma'am. We need to speak to the manager," Sam said.

"His Holiness is busy," the bison rumbled as she leaned down to inspect their badges.

"It's important, ma'am. A beaver was murdered and this store was the last place he was seen alive." Sam tucked her badge away as the bison snorted.

"I'll let him know you're here." The bison stomped over to a phone hidden in the wall. She spoke softly into it for several moments before hanging up and returning to the detectives. She clutched a pink velvet rope, which separated the employee-only area from the general areas, and lifted it up. "His Holiness will see you. Go up the stairs, first door on the right."

As they went up the stairs, Parker whispered in her ear, "wonder if His Holiness has a *glory* hole? Get it?"

Sam groaned and pushed Parker away. "Please, can you save the dirty jokes for later? We need this guy to cooperate with us."

"I'll try, but I make no promises." Parker winked at her and skipped up the last few steps.

The stairs opened into a hallway decorated entirely in

shades of pink. Sam grimaced at the color as Parker knocked.

"Enter," a smooth baritone purred.

Parker opened the door to reveal a cougar in a crisp, pink suit sitting behind a marble desk. The walls were filled with plaques and photos of the cougar in the full Voodoo regalia, pink pillbox hat rakishly askew, posing with a variety of celebrities and politicians of every species.

Sam waddled in and held up a photograph of Dillon. "Good evening, Your Holiness. We are investigating the murder of this beaver, Dillon Dam. He visited here in the early hours of the morning three days ago, shortly before he was killed. We need to talk to the clerk that served him."

The cougar laced his paws together in front of him and contemplated the beaver and raccoon standing before his desk. "This is the busiest Voodoo Donuts in the nation, serving thousands of customers every hour. I'm not sure how helpful the clerk may or may not be. What sort of information are you looking for?"

"We know the victim was here right before he died, but what we don't know for sure is who he was meeting with."

The cat smiled, revealing gleaming white incisors. "Ah. And do you have a warrant?"

Parker handed the cougar a piece of paper he had pulled from his jacket. He *had* been busy this evening before she'd gotten in. Smart raccoon.

His Holiness unfolded the document and placed a pair of reading glasses on his muzzle before peering at it. "Everything looks in order here." He placed the paper on his desk and turned to his computer. After a few moments of typing he rotated the monitor to face Parker and Sam.

The video was shot from behind the counter, at a high angle looking down on the customers. Dillon, wearing the suit he'd been found in, was there with a female beaver. The family resemblance was uncanny. It had to be his sister. She was dressed up for a night on the town, too, with understated but expensive jewelry.

Dillon and his sister were talking, but the video itself was silent. The girl's whiskers twitched and her eyes narrowed. Dillon kept emphatically shaking his head in response to whatever she was saying. The fight seemed to be put on hold as they were served by a vixen. Finally, they waddled out of range of the camera, Dillon clutching their pink box of donuts.

"Your Holiness, can you print a still of the girl he is with?" Sam asked.

"Of course." Behind him a printer whirred and a moment later he handed Sam a glossy color photo of Dillon and his sister.

"We also need to speak with the fox that served them," Sam said.

"You're in luck, she is working this evening." The cougar picked up a phone and spoke in hushed tones to the person on the other end before hanging up. "She'll be up momentarily."

While they waited, Sam studied the photo. Dillon and his sister stood out in their finery amongst the other casually dressed patrons. Various animals of all size and colors snaked out in the line behind the two beavers. A splash of blond fur in the far edge of the background caught her eye, but the figure was mostly hidden in the shadow of a hippo in front of him.

Several long minutes later a timid knock sounded on the outer door before it creaked open. "You wanted to see me, Your Holiness?" The red fox took timid steps into the room, her muzzle pointed to the floor, her ears and tail down in a gesture of submission.

"These detectives have some questions for you about a pair of beavers who visited the store the night before last. Answer them to the best of your ability." His Holiness gave the fox a serene smile and gestured to the detectives.

The fox nodded, but wrung her paws together. "I'll try, Your Holiness, but we see a lot of mammals each night."

"Just do your best," the cougar assured her.

Sam held up the photo the cougar had just printed out. "Do you remember these beavers? Well dressed, arguing as they approached the counter to take communion?"

The fox's ears pricked forward, the black tips tall as she took a long look at the picture. "I remember them," she said finally. "The clothes, I mean. A lot of animals dress up to visit mecca here, but they were a cut above the rest."

"Did you hear what they were arguing about?" Sam pressed.

The fox started to shake her head, then stopped, considering. "Um, well, I was mostly looking at her jewelry, but I think I remember hearing something about a funeral."

Sam set the picture down and jotted notes on her pad, frowning. A funeral would mean a will, and perhaps even an inheritance. "Anything else you can tell us about them?"

"Their accents were posh, I guess." The fox shrugged, helpless, her ears flattening.

"Accents? Posh?" Sam blinked in confusion, her expression echoed on Parker's face next to her.

"Yeah." The fox spread her black paws. "Posh, like you hear on the BBC."

Sam picked up the picture of Dillon and his sister, suddenly realizing what her intuition had been trying to tell her. England. They were European beavers! No wonder something about them had seemed off. It explained the thinner fur and the proportions just different enough from her own to stand out to her. With that extra push, Sam knew exactly who Dillon was.

"Thank you for your help." Sam tucked her notebook and the photo into her pocket and headed for the door. "Sorry to rush out like this but we have a hot lead to follow."

Parker had to have been surprised by Sam's sudden departure, but he kept his questions to himself until they were back in the patrol car.

"Okay, you obviously figured something out. Spill it," Parker said, his eyes bright against his black fur mask as he started up the car.

"I know who Dillon is and why he might have been killed." Sam took a deep breath and blew it out. "I blame the bloating from the water as to why I missed it earlier. Dillon is a European beaver."

"Why does that matter?" Confusion pulled at Parker's face. "And how does that tell you who he is?"

"All us beavers subscribe to news alerts about other beavers. Because most other species can't tell European and American beavers apart, or don't care about the difference, we all get lumped in together."

Parker nodded. "Raccoons get that too."

"There's more than one type of raccoon?" Sam flashed Parker a grin so he'd know she was joking before she continued. "Well, last week, the day before Rick said Dillon got a call from his sister, there was an obituary that came through the feed, for a rich, influential English beaver. It mentioned a surviving son and daughter."

"Wonder why no one else mentioned the accent?" Parker mused.

"We didn't ask about it, so they probably didn't think it relevant. First things first, we need to talk to Dillon's sister. As of now, she was the last person to see Dillon alive. Now that we know who she is it shouldn't take long to locate her," Sam said.

Once they got to the station, a quick internet search pulled up the obituary Sam had remembered. A few clicks later got her to another article about the deceased that included a picture of the grieving family at the funeral. Sam recognized the female beaver as the one in the printout from Voodoo. This article included a name for Dillon's sister, Eugenia Carpenter.

"What now?" Parker asked from over her shoulder.

Sam handed him a printout of hotels around Portland, sorted with the priciest at the top of the list. "Now we start calling."

As Sam reached for her phone to call hotels it began to ring, so she answered it. "Hello. This is Detective Digger."

Parker glanced at her, his masked face alight with curiosity.

"Hi Detective," a dog barked. "This is Ozzy Waggeth, from the Lucky Lab?"

"Yes, how can I help you?" Sam covered up the mouthpiece and mouthed "Ozzy" at Parker, who nodded.

"I-I have something to tell you about Dillon's murder. I mean, I really liked Dillon. I know he had the hots for me, he was always flirting with me. It's a shame what happened. I…" She could hear the hesitation in his voice. "I didn't want to say anything in front of Dave, but, well, you should take a closer look at that human, Rick."

"Oh, why's that?"

"Well, when Dillon didn't show up for his shift the other night I helped cover the bar. Rick got pretty wasted that night and said something about being sorry."

"Sorry for what?" Sam pressed.

"I don't know," the dog sounded apologetic. "But I thought you should know. Gotta go."

The phone beeped off before Sam could respond.

"What was that about?" Parker asked.

"I have no idea." Sam shook her head. "Ozzy pointing a claw at Rick for this murder. You call hotels. I'm going to call Rick and ask him about what Ozzy just said."

Sam dialed Rick's number. The phone rang and rang with no answer.

Concerned, she hung up, double-checked the phone number—she'd had it right—and dialed again. Again, there was no answer.

Parker looked at her, curiosity making his whiskers twitch.

"Rick's not answering and I'm getting worried," Sam told him.

"Good thing I was a busy little beaver this morning." Parker grinned.

Sam shot him an irritated glare. Parker knew she hated that particular expression. "Meaning?"

"I got us a warrant to search Dillon's room. Let the rookies handle calling the hotels while we execute our warrant," Parker said with a wink.

***

As they entered the quiet, residential neighborhood Parker turned off the siren, but left on the lights. The flashing red and blue gave the place an abandoned feel as it illuminated children's toys left in yards, parked cars, and dark windows. Primarily a human neighborhood, most of the houses were dark and quiet, their residents sleeping, leaving the night to the nocturnals. Their destination was obvious as soon as they turned onto the street; the lights in the house blazed like a beacon.

Sam was already unbuckling her seat belt as Parker pulled the car to a stop in front of the house. She was waddling up the walk before he'd even put the car into park. Something was wrong. Rick was human and he hadn't mentioned any other roommates. He hadn't answered his phone so he might have been sleeping, yet the lights were on.

Parker caught up with her as she navigated up the concrete steps to the door, the nimbler raccoon scrambling up the large steps in a couple of hops. At the top Sam belatedly noticed a small black ramp set to the side of the steps that curved around to the grass; probably to assist Dillon in entering and exiting the human-sized dwelling.

While Parker jumped into the air to ring the doorbell, Sam stood on tiptoes to peer in the picture window that looked out onto the porch. Inside, the living room was empty and she could just see into a small corner of the kitchen. As Parker knocked on the door, a pair of human legs and shoes briefly swung into view next to the kitchen counter.

"Rick's hung himself!" Sam swore and grabbed one of the porch planters. She lifted it overhead and heaved it at the window. The planter smashed through with a crash, sending broken glass scattering into the house.

Parker jumped through the opening ahead of Sam while she pulled herself inside, the glass tearing at her front paws as she struggled to climb in. By the time she crawled down from the couch and waddled into the kitchen, Parker had already nimbly climbed Rick's limp form and was sawing at the rope with his claws. Sam pushed an overturned chair out of the way and moved underneath, ready to catch the human. Rick's face was blue and his hands twitched feebly where they clutched at the rope around his neck. They'd gotten to him in time.

"Head's up!" Parker called as the rope gave way with a sharp snap.

Rick's limp body dropped onto Sam while Parker leapt away onto the counter. She let his feet and butt hit the kitchen floor, catching him around the chest. His weight, even just the top half of him, threatened to topple her. She dropped him and pulled the limp rope from his neck, tossing it away. Rick rolled over, gagging and retching while Parker nimbly jumped off the counter.

"What were you thinking?" Sam growled at the prone human.

Rick didn't answer, instead he curled into a ball and sobbed fitfully. Sam sighed and pulled out her phone while Parker attempted to comfort the human.

An apathetic voice answered. "Dispatch."

"We went to execute a warrant and interrupted a suicide by hanging. Victim is alive and conscious, but hurt. Send an ambulance over to—" Sam pulled out her notebook and read off Rick's address. When she was done she waddled back to the kitchen.

"Why'd you stop me?" Rick croaked into his hands. "Nothing matters anymore now that Dillon's gone." His words dissolved into shuddering sobs, his shoulders shaking.

"Everything will be okay," Parker murmured and patted Rick's shoulder even as he looked up at Sam, a frown pulling down his whiskers.

"Ambulance is on its way. Be here in five," Sam told him. Now that Rick was safe she examined the house. Everything was human sized, with marble countertops and plaster walls. The kitchen was neat and clean, decorated with happy cartoon beavers. The only sign of Dillon's presence was a folding step stool propped in the corner and a log in the corner with half its bark gnawed off.

Sam left Rick in Parker's care and wandered into the living room. Framed photographs of humans hung on the walls high above Sam's head and more frames clustered together on the end tables. Rick's family, if she didn't miss her guess. Interspersed among them were pictures of Rick and Dillon together: Rick and Dillon at the stadium, Rick and Dillon having a picnic at the park, Rick and Dillon posing in front of Willamette Falls. Sam scratched behind an ear with one paw as she walked a circuit of the living room.

From the kitchen she could hear Parker still comforting Rick, the situation well under control. She left the living room and headed down the hall.

The first door was open, showing a cramped bathroom. Human and beaver grooming products littered the counter. The door opposite the bathroom led to a study stuffed with bookcases and two desks, one sized for humans and one for mammals of Sam, Parker, and Dillon's size. Enough moonlight came through the window to show her that the chair behind the small desk had a cut-out backrest shaped like a C, built especially for beavers to accommodate their wide, flat tails.

An open cardboard box sat in the hall just in front of the last door. Sam peered cautiously inside and discovered it was full of letters. Sam picked one up and started to read it. *All that I am, all that I see is brighter because of you. Just the smell of your fur leaves me breathless. No one loves you like I do.* Sam recoiled with a scowl. How creepy. She turned her attention back to the last door.

Sam frowned, slapping her tail on the carpet. She closed her eyes. It couldn't be. It just couldn't. Maybe that creepy love poem had been from Rick to Dillon. She opened her eyes and reflexively groomed her whiskers. Might as well check it out.

Whiskers twitching, Sam pushed open the door and stepped through into the dark bedroom. Beaver musk and human sweat stung her nose, confirming the two spent a lot of time here. The drapes had been drawn, leaving the room in a deep twilight so thick even Sam's vision couldn't penetrate it. With the house being human-sized in construction the light switches would be above her head, out of easy groping reach, so Sam pulled out her flashlight and clicked it on. After a few moments of shining the light around near the door she located the switch. She had to stretch to reach it. Sam blinked, blinded by the overhead light as it winked on, but at least now she could examine the room.

A single large bed dominated the center of the room, facing a large flat-screen TV on a stand. The TV was on but the image had been paused on a shot of a smiling Dillon standing in this very bedroom. Rick had been watching a home movie of Dillon before going out and hanging himself in the kitchen.

The closet doors stood open, the inside a mishmash of beaver and human clothing. A plastic tub, its lid askew, sat on the floor by the end of the bed. More framed pictures dotted the wall in here, but rather than portraits and candid fun shots, these showed lots of bare human skin and uncovered fur. Sam couldn't stop her muzzle from falling open as she gaped at the carnal images.

Morbid curiosity made her go up to the paused DVD player and press play. On-screen Dillon moved, sauntering forward with an unnatural swagger as he began a dancing striptease for the camera.

"Oh, yeah, take it all off." The voice came from off camera, but Sam recognized it as Rick's.

Dillon grinned, turning his back to the camera and bending over to shimmy out of his pants. "You like that baby?" He growled in a passable American drawl. He tossed the garment aside and wriggled his naked butt at the camera. Well, that answered the question of why no one had mentioned a British accent. Dillion really was quite handsome.

A naked human male entered the camera frame. Sam squealed, averting her eyes as she darted forward to stop the show. That was more than she'd ever wanted to see of any human, ever. It also confirmed something else. Dillon and Rick were lovers.

***

The loud wail of a siren could be heard as Sam emerged from the bedroom. She had a feeling the paramedics would object to her questioning Rick with his throat hurt like it was, but she needed answers.

"Rick," Sam said as she entered the kitchen. The human was sitting up now, resting his head on drawn-up knees, arms wrapped around his legs. He glanced at her. "How long have you and Dillon been partners?"

Parker blinked at her in surprise. To be honest Sam still didn't quite believe it herself, even with what she'd seen.

"You saw...?" Rick grimaced. "Don't tell, please."

"How long, Rick?"

He sighed. "Two years."

"Ozzy mentioned Dillon fighting with another patron, a human, about six months ago. Do you know anything about that?"

"Yeah, Dillon cheated. I caught him, we fought about it. I told Dillon if he didn't stop seeing that guy I'd kick him out." Rick broke off into a fit of coughing.

"But the guy didn't take it well," Sam finished for him.

Rick nodded.

The siren was growing closer with each second. She didn't have much time left.

"Do you think Dillon was cheating on you again?" Sam pressed him.

"I had... suspected it." Rick hugged his knees tight. "But he wasn't, and now I can never tell him I'm sorry."

Sam suppressed a sigh. So that was what Ozzy had overheard.

"So, you wrote Dillon those love letters trying to get him

back."

Rick shuddered and shook his head. "No. God no. Someone kept leaving those awful things for Dillon. We called the police, but they wouldn't do anything unless the letters directly threatened us. I was saving them as evidence, in case it went that far." Rick coughed, his voice getting raspy. It was obviously hurting him to talk. "We got the last one the night before Dillon died."

"But none after?" Sam hated having to make him talk more, but it might be important.

Rick shook his head again.

"Rick, do you know where Dillon went the night he died?" Sam asked quietly.

Tears streamed down Rick's cheeks. "No."

Flashing blue lights from the front of the house told her the ambulance had arrived. She gestured to Parker to stay with Rick as she went to open the door for the paramedics. The driver, a female black bear, popped out of the cab, spotted Sam standing in the doorway, and waved at her. A German shepherd and a long-haired collie got out of the back carrying a stretcher between them.

As the dogs carried the stretcher through the door Sam pointed to the kitchen. "In there."

It only took a few minutes for the paramedics to look Rick over and declare their intentions to take him to the hospital. Sam and Parker saw them off, watching the ambulance until it was out of sight. Once it was gone Parker turned to her, his eyes blazing with curiosity.

"A human-beaver couple. I never would have guessed." Parker said it matter of fact, then gestured to the empty house. "Might as well execute our search warrant before we leave."

It turned out that Sam had already found pretty much all there was to find. They entered the DVD into evidence, along with the box of creepy letters from Dillon's stalker.

They got back into the car. The light mist had turned into a downpour. Parker turned on the car and wipers, but didn't put the car into gear. "It wasn't Rick."

"I know," Sam sighed and lay her head back against the seats headrest. "Your rookies have any luck with those hotel lists?"

Parker held up his phone. "Yup. He just texted me. Eugenia is staying at The Heathman, downtown."

***

Twenty minutes later they pushed through the revolving doors into the lobby of the Historic Heathman. Sam drooled at all the polished dark-wood paneling. At this late hour of the night the lobby was empty except for a hound porter lounging in one of the chairs and a bored-looking human manning the front desk.

As they approached the front desk, the human straightened and leaned over the counter so he could speak with them. "Hello, can I help you?"

"Yes, sir." Sam squinted up at the man's name tag. "John, I'm Detective Digger and this is my partner, Detective Ringschein. We called a little bit ago about Eugenia Carpenter."

"Oh, hello." John pulled back, disappearing behind the tall counter. Keys clacked as he typed at his computer. "I'll just need to see your badges and then I'll inform Miss Carpenter of your arrival."

"Yes, here." Sam stretched on her tiptoes and held her badge above the counter.

"May I ask what you need to speak with her regarding?" John asked.

"It's about her brother."

A phone clicked and John spoke quietly into it for a moment before hanging up. "Miss Carpenter has agreed to speak to you. Room 1009, on the tenth floor."

Sam waddled toward the elevators, Parker at her heels, snapping bubbles in his nicotine gum. The lounging hound looked up as they passed him, cocking a curious ear at them.

They rode up in silence, each lost in their own whirring

thoughts until the elevator dinged quietly and the doors slid open. The upstairs was decorated in the same style as the lobby, lots of dark wood, paintings of humans and dogs in outdoor scenes, and burgundy carpeting.

The hotel served mainly humans and canines, and at this late hour the halls were as quiet as a ghost town. Sam stepped up to room 1009 and rapped sharply.

"Who is it?" said a low female voice with a heavy English accent from the other side.

"Portland P.D., ma'am. We need to ask you a few questions," Sam said.

The locks on the other side of the door rattled and the door clicked open to reveal the gorgeous female beaver from the Voodoo surveillance video. She wore a pair of lacy pajamas covered by a robe.

Sam stepped forward slightly. "Miss Carpenter, I'm Detective Digger and this is Detective Ringschein." Sam gestured to herself and then to Parker. "May we come in?"

Eugenia Carpenter frowned and pulled her robe tighter. "No, you may not. We can talk here. The front desk said you were here about my brother?"

Sam took a deep breath. "I'm sorry to tell you this, but Dillon is dead."

"What?" Eugenia's eyes widened and her muzzle gaped. She staggered back to a resting position on her tail. "What happened?"

"Can we come in? I'd rather not discuss this in the hall," Sam said.

"Of course." Eugenia left the door open and turned, shuffling farther into the room.

Sam and Parker followed in after her, shutting the door behind them. Eugenia sank into the plush chair in the corner, her tail stuck out under her feet. Parker pulled over the desk chair, while Sam just settled back onto her own tail.

Eugenia suddenly looked very tired, her black eyes sunken and her whiskers drooping. She groomed the fur on her arm in a nervous gesture, not looking at the two detectives.

"Dillon was found dead early yesterday evening, floating in the river," Sam said, breaking the tense silence. "He was murdered."

"That explains why he wasn't returning my calls." Eugenia shuddered, her paws tightening.

"When was the last time you saw Dillon?" Parker asked.

"Here." Eugenia gestured at her room. "On Saturday night. Dillon and I had a long talk. He left here early in the morning."

"Early in the morning? About what time, would you say?" Sam pressed her.

Eugenia wrinkled her muzzle, twitching back one rounded ear. "Before dawn. I didn't pay attention to the time."

"Do you know where your brother went when he left here?" Sam asked.

Eugenia blinked in surprise. "Next door, of course. He had the adjoining room."

Sam resisted slapping her tail in frustration, but just barely. "Uh, okay. Did anything happen or did you hear anything from next door after Dillon left?" Sam said.

"No," Eugenia said with a shrug.

Eugenia didn't even seem fazed by news of her brother's death. "Miss Carpenter, what were you and Dillon fighting about at Voodoo?" Sam might as well get this over with.

Eugenia gave a little start and looked directly at Sam for the first time. "How did you know about that?"

"We're detectives, Miss Carpenter. We investigated. What were you fighting about?"

"My father's funeral." Eugenia bared her teeth, her eyes glittering with rage. "Dillon couldn't even be bothered to attend."

"You flew all the way out here, just to tell him that?"

"No. I came out here to convince him to come back for the reading of the will," Eugenia said. "My father specified that both of us must be present. Dillon didn't want to come, even for that, so I flew out here to appeal to him in person."

"So, I take it Dillon turned you down?" Sam hazarded a

guess.

"Yes, that's why I'm still in this godforsaken town. I can't go back without him. After our talk Dillon said he'd think about it, but then he never returned my calls."

"You didn't try to look for him?" Parker said.

Eugenia grimaced. "Of course I did. I went by his hovel, but his slut said he hadn't been home. I called the private investigator that found him for me in the first place, but he was unable to track him down again. So this evening I reported him missing."

"Is Dillon set to inherit any money?" Sam asked.

Eugenia averted her eyes. "I don't know."

"But you suspect your father might have left it all to Dillon?"

"Yes!" Eugenia bared her teeth and slid out of the chair. "But it is just that, a suspicion. Now, detectives, I've told you everything I know. If there isn't anything else, I have some calls to make and another funeral to arrange."

She walked Sam and Parker to the door, slamming it behind them. Parker pulled his tail out of the way with a yelp. On the other side there was the sound of deadbolts sliding into place.

"Well, that wasn't highly suspicious or anything," Parker muttered, hugging his tail to his chest.

***

The elevator ride down to the lobby was silent; both Sam and Parker were lost in their own thoughts. After stepping into the lobby Sam approached John at the front desk again.

"Hello again, Detective." The human looked down over the counter at them. "What can I do for you now?"

"We need to take a look at the room adjoining to Eugenia's, number 1011," Sam said.

John looked surprised. "What, why?"

"Her brother, Dillon, was staying there the night he was murdered." Might as well be upfront with him.

John's eyes widened and he flushed. "Murder? I—oh my. I think housekeeping would have noticed something like that." John vanished behind the counter and Sam could hear the clack of a keyboard. "It looks like Dillon left without checking out, but since the room had only been booked through Saturday night it was cleaned and reoccupied."

Sam twitched her whiskers. She suspected it was a deadend, but they still couldn't account for Dillon's whereabouts from when he'd left Eugenia's room until he'd been killed. If, in fact, Eugenia had been telling them the truth.

"They've already cleaned the room and had other guests in it," Parker said as he shoved a fresh stick of nicotine gum into his mouth. "What do you think we'll find there?"

Sam shrugged and twitched her whiskers. "Probably nothing. But we should check it out anyway."

"I see," John answered. He'd leaned back over the counter and now pursed his lips as he regarded them. "We have guests in there right now. I'm sorry but I'm going to have to ask for a warrant as we must respect our guest's privacy."

"We don't have a warrant yet," Sam admitted.

"Then come back when you get one." John pulled back out of sight.

"Wait!" Sam called. John leaned back over. "Was anything left in 1011 when it was cleaned?"

"Let me check." He disappeared and his footsteps retreated into a back room.

Parker pulled out his cell phone. "You take a look at what he brings out; I'm going to call about that warrant."

Parker walked off, his phone to his ear. A few moments later John came around the desk carrying a small plastic tub. He laid the bin on the floor by Sam's feet and retreated behind the counter.

The tub was empty except for a neatly folded pair of beaver-sized jeans and a plaid top, similar to the one Dillon had been wearing in his missing persons photo. Sam snapped a few photos of the clothing before she pulled it out. The only other item in the tub was Dillon's wallet. Sam picked it up and flipped through it. It was stuffed with ones and fives, probably the tips he'd made during his last shift at the Lucky Lab. Dillon's ID was still in its little plastic sleeve, and a dozen credit cards were stacked together in the slots.

Parker came back as Sam was preparing the last of the evidence bags. "Judge is signing it now. We should have it in just a few more minutes," he said, bright eyes flicking around the bags spread about on the floor. "Anything?"

Sam flicked an ear and gestured at the bags. "Notice anything missing?"

"Hmm...wallet, clothes, ID. No surprise there. We'd already ruled out robbery."

Sam nodded. "But his overnight bag isn't here."

Parker's eyes lit up for a moment, flashing in his mask, but then he frowned. "Why leave his phone, an expensive watch, credit cards, and cash, but take his suitcase?"

"No idea." Sam sighed. "Help me carry this stuff to the car."

***

John was sour when they walked back into the lobby a few hours later with the warrant, but he had a key card waiting for them. "We've moved the guests from that room to a new one, so feel free to take your time. Let me know when you are done."

Parker and Sam made their way upstairs in silence, both lost in thought. When they got to the room Sam slipped the keycard into the lock and entered without bothering to put on gloves. Since the room had already been cleaned and reoccupied, they weren't likely to find any useful prints.

It was a typical hotel room, although it was much more opulent than any hotel room she'd ever been able to afford. It showed signs of recent use. The covers of the large bed were thrown back, the drawers halfway open, and the plush chair in the corner was askew. Sam ignored the bedroom and turned into the bathroom. They knew he'd drowned and the bathroom was the only logical place that could have happened.

A long counter and a sink dominated the left side of the room. The right side of the room was filled with a human-sized bathtub. Long scratches marred its edges. Sam held up her paw and compared it to the marks. Dillon definitely could have made these.

Sam pulled out her black light and shone it along the edge. Small dots shone luminescent in the harsh light on either side of the scratches. She took out a cotton swab and carefully dabbed at one of the spots, capped it, and put it into an evidence bag. "I'd say we've found the scene of the murder."

Parker looked over her shoulder and frowned. "But Dillon wasn't hurt, where did that blood come from?"

Sam held up a paw and hooked her fingers. "People forget that cute little beavers have rather sharp claws." That gave her pause. "Did Rick have marks on his arm?"

Parker cocked his head to the side. "No," he said finally. "Marks like that stand out on humans' bare skin."

"Well, that eliminates one suspect." Sam sighed. "That leaves, who, the sister? But, no. It can't be her."

"It has to be," Parker said, scratching his chin. "She's the only one with means. She kills him, dumps him in the river, and goes back to her room. All the rest of our suspects weren't in the hotel. They didn't even know where Dillon was."

Sam shook her head, her mind connecting the pieces of the puzzle. "Yes, they did. It all fits." Sam turned to Parker with a grin as they left the hotel room. "Let's go arrest our murderer."

***

Parker pulled the car up in front of the Lucky Lab just as the sun peaked above the horizon. The sound of their doors slamming was loud in the pre-dawn silence.

The Lab was quiet as they approached and filed in through

the doors. Inside, the bar was empty of patrons. No one was visible at the bar, but the sound of clinking glasses came from behind the employee-only door at the far end.

Sam rapped on the low bar. "Hello, anyone here?"

"Bar's closed." Ozzy's golden-furred form came backing out of the employee door with a cloud of steam hissing around him. He turned, lugging a load of clean glasses over to the bar.

"Oh, hello detectives!" Ozzy's tail wagged and his tongue lolled out as he set the load down with a tinkle of chiming glass. "Dave's gone home for the morning, but I can give him a call if you'd like."

"No, Ozzy." Sam took out her handcuffs and laid them on the bar. "We're here to arrest you for the murder of Dillon Dam. Put your paws in the air."

"Me?" Ozzy stared at the handcuffs, his eyes widening. "But I'm the one that reported Dillon missing."

"Give up the act, Ozzy. You followed Dillon that night. You drowned him in the bathtub of his own hotel room, stuffed him into his overnight bag, walked down to the docks, and dumped him in the river." Sam picked up the handcuffs. "Now, are you going to come quietly?"

Ozzy's ears drooped and he put his paws in the air. "How?"

"You were stalking Dillon. We have you in the background of the security footage of Voodoo Donuts and you have scratches on your arm where Dillon fought back while you drowned him in the tub." Sam shook her head as she snapped on the cuffs. "Such a waste."

The rain picked up, drumming loudly on the roof of the Lucky Lab.

"I love him," Ozzy sobbed. "I did it for us." Ozzy had to stop and take a shuddering breath. "For *us.*" Ozzy's dismayed howling nearly deafened her, louder even than the rain.

***

Sam was glad they'd caught the killer, but it was such a waste.

A life gone, one of a beaver in his prime. A dog who'd go to prison for the rest of his life. A broken-hearted human.

Sam, who before this case hadn't given humans much thought and had actively avoided them on the streets, was suddenly overcome with worry for Rick. He'd lost his mate to this senseless tragedy. Even worse, poor Rick wouldn't even get to attend Dillon's funeral. His remains would be released to Eugenia and returned to Europe for burial in the family crypt. On a whim, she asked Parker what she could bring a human to cheer them up.

Parker zipped up his coat and wagged his tail. "You planning to visit Rick?"

Sam nodded, wringing her front paws together in embarrassment.

"C'mon, I know just the thing." Parker grinned, his black eyes sparkling.

***

The arrived at the hospital just as visiting hours for diurnal creatures started. A Bulldog nurse showed them into Rick's room.

Rick was lying listlessly in bed, staring out the window. When they entered he didn't even glance at them, until one of Parker's cubs scrambled up the sheets and plopped herself down in Rick's lap.

"Hi, my name's Maggie," she yipped, her little tail wagging under her dress.

Rick glanced down at Maggie in surprise, his eyes going wide. Finally he looked up and took note of Sam, standing in the doorway with Parker and his wife, Stacy. The raccoon couple were busy trying to corral the rest of the cubs, who all wanted to join Maggie in Rick's lap.

"Hi, I, uh, got these for you." Sam waddled forward and gave Rick a bundle of flowers Sam wasn't sure why humans would want flowers, they tasted quite awful, but Parker had been adamant that Rick would like them.

"We caught the killer. He'll be in prison for the rest of his life, and he'll never be able to hurt anyone like this ever again," Sam said gravely.

At first Rick just stared down, his eyes flicking between the flowers and the raccoon cub happily bouncing around in his lap. Parker and Stacey lost the fight. A moment later Maggie was joined by three more prancing cubs, all clamoring about in Rick's lap, jabbering for attention. The corner of Rick's mouth turned up, and he let out a hiccupping laugh.

"Thank you," he said, giving them all a sad smile. "For everything."

FROST BRIDGE

Amethystos

BERING STRAIT

The crisp autumn air crept between Sybil's feathers, and the sparrow shivered. Now was the time to take flight and soar south until the sun became tall in the sky and her feathers grew warmer. Yet, she could not bear to open her wings. Her pride would not allow her. She looked out across the forested mountains and their sweeping hills. The mist that had settled in this valley smelled of the sea. She grew ever closer to the ocean with each passing moment. There, the water would keep the temperatures a bit more tolerable.

Her legs burned from climbing so long, but she pressed on anyways. The coast would be warmer than the rest of Siberia and the comfortable temperatures would give her time to think. Should she journey south? Should she brave the way, all on foot? Even if she started now, the biting winds of winter would catch up to her. Part of her looked at these mountains and knew she would never see them again. Another part of her awoke every now and then, filling her with determination and a desire to head south, no matter the chances of survival.

Sybil dug her talons into the earth, straining with each step to reach the top of the mountain. The sea was close, so very close. She rounded the peak and gazed out across the landscape. Instead of water, she saw a plain of ice, with bright blue glaciers striking up at the sky where the sea waves had pushed them out. She collapsed, drawing her legs into her feathers and hugging her wings close to her. The waters she knew were warm and inviting, with tropical growth crowding the edges of the sea. She never stayed long enough to see the sea itself freeze over—tales of such a feat seemed like a fable.

Now more than ever, she felt just how far she should have flown and just how close death was. She shut her eyes and shuddered. Even as the sun ducked below the clouds, the light it brought did not warm her. Nothing would warm her again.

She lay quiet for a time, feeling the air grow colder around her as the sun set. Perhaps it would frost tonight. The winter had taken its time this year, but already the ice extended as far out as the eye could see. Was this all a mistake? No. She knew what would happen the moment she didn't heed the falling leaves. The thin clothes she wore did nothing to stave off the chill. She felt herself slipping into torpor, darkness closing in around her. She faintly wondered if she would ever see him again.

***

"Are you rousing?" asked a gruff voice.

Sybil jolted awake, her feathers flooded with warmth again. The horizon was glowing with a faint light—perhaps a few hours before sunrise. She shook her feathers to heat up, pulling off an unfamiliar blanket to take advantage of a bonfire lit close to her. She moved the blanket away, exposing the flight feathers on her wrist to the warm air. Heat started flowing through her veins. Her eyes adjusted to the contrast and made out a large figure—perhaps twice her size—sitting across from her. Curved horns jutted upwards and out from his brow, and his black muzzle and white fur instantly gave away his species. An elk. An herbivore. She was safe another night.

The elk gazed into her open eyes and nodded. "If you weren't, then I suppose you are now. Perhaps too cold to speak?" He poked at the fire and picked out a golden roll of some sort. He tossed it to her and she caught it in her taloned fingers. "I made you some piroshky. Hopefully it's to your taste. I'm not certain if you like meat or not, so I just went with my usual recipe."

He picked out another bun and bit into it. She could see crisp cabbage, roasted seeds, bits of potato and onion, and some strange green stuff that resembled lichen. The delicious smell floated into her nares, and although her stomach knotted with the thought of eating, she took a few nibbles of the bun. The warmth flowed through her and she finally stopped shivering. "This cabbage is sweet," she mumbled between bites.

"Yes, the frost makes cabbage sweet in the winter. Though I don't suppose a sparrow would know... No, a sparrow should not know." He adopted a stern voice. "What are you doing here? I thought you were dead—I wasn't even sure if you were breathing, and your body was terribly cold. If I had been a predator, you would not be waking now. I only saved you because the frost had not formed on you yet."

"Thank you," Sybil said quietly. "It was torpor—when it gets too cold, I fall asleep, and my body gets as cold as the air. I wake up whenever it warms again. When the nights grow longer, I spend more time in that darker sleep."

"Ah," sighed the elk, with a small tinge of relief in his voice. He looked out towards the horizon, where light was slowly growing. "The sun rises later and later this year. The equinox already passed. We don't know if tomorrow comes with warmth. The clouds grow ever more present, and yet a sparrow like you has not flown south yet. You must migrate, little one. What hinders you?"

"Well..." Sybil searched for the right words. She drew a circle in the ground with a talon. "My wings fly no longer, so I came to the sea instead. I was hoping for warm water, not... all this ice."

"Oh. I'm sorry." He sounded flustered. He looked at her wings carefully, and she returned the gaze. Gray fur mixed in around his muzzle, ears, and hands betrayed his age. Those eyes would not be fooled. "Your wings seem unharmed."

She stretched out her feathers in a small display, contemplating her answer. "The worst wounds inflict no mark on the body."

He seemed satisfied by the answer. At the very least, he did not prod further. Although he wore clothes with deep dyes and elegant embroidery, the fabric was worn thin and filled with dark green stains. His horns rose high and split into many prongs, but they were covered in a thin white film and flaking in some parts.

"Oh no, those antlers!" she gasped. "I'm so sorry, but I don't have any medicine for them. My wares were too heavy to carry for so long, but—Oh, I suppose I could make you some new medicine! An ointment to smooth out your—"

He waved a dismissive hand. "Never mind my horns. They will fall off before winter sets in and return in the spring. That's the natural way of things." He looked at her curiously now. "You sold medicine? What is your name?"

"I'm called Sybil Windbrooke. I used to sell medicines. When I could fly, I learned about medicines all over the world. I was happy to learn as much as I could and spread that knowledge everywhere I went. Each summer and autumn, I would carry rare medicines farther than any trading routes went, but that was all before…well, my flight."

The elk nodded. "I understand. You put your wings to good use when you flew, so be proud. My name is Dmitri. Just Dmitri. I have lived on these cliffs for many years, helping my own kind with their migrations. Predators lurk everywhere in the summer months, but they tolerate me. Perhaps they will tolerate you."

"Tolerate me? What do you mean?" she asked.

"You will not make it to your fair weather by walking. You will have to remain here, in these icy lands, but I would like you to stay with me. I'm in need of assistance, and I can offer you food and shelter until spring arrives. When this land is no longer frozen, you should head south until the heat becomes tolerable and remain there, where winter does not bite."

Sybil stopped drawing in the dirt and stared at him warily. "What sort of work?"

"I need a small house built before the first snow. Right now, I live in this outcropping, but would prefer a roof over my head. Since you know your medicine, I would like a stock of any you can make. Many guests travel through these lands, and my job is to care for them and ensure their safety as best I can."

Dmitri stood up as the first red rays of light hit the pine trees around them. "I understand that the urge to migrate might be strong, but with no way to fly, you must find another way to survive." He kneeled down and nudged her piroshky-holding hand closer to her face. "For starters, you must finish your meals."

"My apologies. I do appreciate the meal, and it is tasty, but…" She looked away from his sincere gaze.

"You don't want to help?"

"What can a sparrow like me do? I know nothing of building a home, nor any sort of carpentry."

The elk stood back up on his legs. "Certainly, you can do more than an old elk like me. You will be paid for your work, of course."

She nibbled at her piroshky again. She wasn't worried about payment. She didn't expect to live beyond the first snowfall. And yet, something moved in her. He promised to keep a sparrow alive through the winter, which would be unbelievable, if not for his wizened stature and determination. He actually thought it was possible. Along with that, if he was asking a stray sparrow for help, he likely didn't have anyone else to turn to. She stood up, stretched her long legs and wings, and ate the last bite of her piroshky.

"We can talk about payment in the spring. I'll do what I can."

***

The leaves fell swiftly and their progress on the cabin went just as fast. Sybil's thin legs and frail wings couldn't move heavy logs, so instead she scavenged for Dmitri while he toiled all day. He taught her to find the winter refuge of nuts, lichen, grass, and so on. Throughout the day, she munched on snacks and grubs as she found them, and at the end would carry home wingfuls of food and dry sticks. He taught her how to set a fire—something she never needed to know beforehand—as well as how to roast and cook amazing meals.

The sun rose later and set earlier, shortening her scavenging trips drastically. She couldn't risk falling into torpor where Dmitri could not find her, and the nights were now fatally cold to her. When the log cabin gained its walls, she began to sleep in the shelter. When she woke, she would tell him where she would go searching for food. Sometimes she went to the frozen creek beds, other times into the wind-carved cliffs, or perhaps an open clearing nearby to dig under the snow. But today, she picked her favorite spot to scavenge—the peak where they had met.

The vast view from the mountain top reminded her of days spent flying. During the day, she could see much more than the misty mountains had revealed during her travels. A large glacier sat in the mountainside, atop which a meltwater lake had formed. The water itself was as deep as the sea despite its location on top of the ice. During the night it would form a thin film of ice, and when the sun rose, huge waves would tear the ice to pieces and push it onto the shore. On misty days, the glacier would disappear entirely. She supposed it would freeze over when the cold set in and stay that way until spring. As for today, it stood still and reflected the light of the sky perfectly. Its placid form sent a shiver of fright and intrigue through her body.

Today, she let her mind and eyes wander over the land. The sun had reached its zenith, yet she could still see her breath turn to fog before her, and her shadow stretched for longer than it should have in front of her. Then, movement! A large shadow flowed across the mountains, sweeping into the valley and curving around the glacial lake. As they grew closer, the shadow divided into smaller figures, with every other head bearing sweeping antlers. A herd of elk!

She whisked down the mountain, nearly dropping her collection of food once or twice. She wanted to fly and greet them, but since that idea was clearly not an option, she raced to alert Dmitri of his visitors. The elk was toiling away at the roof's frame. The building was circular, with small windows and a space for a chimney right in the center. The roof was incredibly short and forced him to navigate carefully through the space.

"Dmitri! Visitors! A whole herd of elk just waltzed through the lake valley!"

Instead of looking excited, the elk twitched his ears at her and seemed…disappointed? She couldn't tell. He ducked out of the house, his antlers barely fitting through the door, and spoke. "I was hoping no one would come this year. Come with me, and you'll see what I do in this place."

She tilted her head with curiosity and followed behind him. She had to take two steps for each one of his strides. Instead of going to the lake valley, they journeyed along the edge of the coast towards a region she had never explored. They crossed several footpaths before turning onto a large trail filled with footprints of all sizes and types. She noted that most of them were hoofprints that matched the size of Dmitri's feet. As the trail grew larger, she started to hear the calls and shouts from the herd of elk. Though her eyes couldn't spot them through the forest, they grew louder and closer with each passing moment.

At last they arrived to a large building that looked like something between a house and an inn. Unlike the house she was building with Dmitri, this building had carved wood, painted tiles, and a whole host of square windows. Each window had its own little alcove and a roof extension. Looking in, she could see beds laid close together with thick blankets and fluffy pillows enticing her to crawl in. Dmitri never told her about this place.

She struggled to match his stride and pull up beside him. "Dmitri, what's this?"

He stopped in front of the building and looked back across the path. "A rest point."

Migrating animals used rest points as temporary homes on their long journeys. Residents that did not migrate maintained them and usually made a pretty penny for their service. As a migrator herself, she had been to a few of them, but avoided rest points built without avians in mind. The solid roof and dark interior of this one sparked a little bit of claustrophobia in her, but she set it aside for now. "For elk?"

Dmitri nodded. "I originally thought to take you here, but I knew you would hate the design. Avians never visit."

"Who maintains it? It couldn't be—" She gasped with realization, "You?!"

He nodded again. "I lived here before I met you. My job is to maintain this place and overlook the migration of my fellow elk. Unfortunately, I have another duty to show you today."

"Never mind that! You told me you lived in the grove at the top of the mountains! And that you needed a home. We've been building it for over a month now, and it's nearly done!"

"The home is for you," he replied, silencing her. She looked at him with pure surprise. "You do not intend to fly south again. I can understand that. You lost something very important to you, whether it was your flight or…something else." His gaze seemed to stab into her soul.

"I couldn't leave you to freeze or starve or be devoured here, but I knew you would turn down my offer of shelter. So I lied and said I needed a home, and built one for you instead. A place you could remain safe and call your own, even through the sting of winter. When a beast intends to meet death, their entire demeanor changes, and I recognized the look of acceptance in your eye. I knew a healer like yourself could not turn down a request of a gray muzzle like me and used that to keep your will alive.

"I enjoyed camping and building, and I still intend to finish the home and give it to you. Please, don't hate me for it. And don't think it is entirely out of generosity that I help you. I still need your aid, so please, don't disappear into the snow."

Sybil couldn't summon the words to respond. He was right about many things—she would have died without his intervention and would be reluctant to even step into a building meant for elk with a complete stranger. The home they were building suited her needs much more, with its large hole in the roof that a typical avian could fly from, a prominent fireplace, and its quaint, nest-like size and shape. The matter was one of whether she wanted to live or die. Despite the weeks spent gathering supplies and growing closer to Dmitri, she still wasn't sure about that. What did he really need help with?

He interrupted before she could conjure up a reply. "We can talk about that later. For now, we have guests. Listen carefully."

She looked back down the path and saw the herd of elk approaching, all different sizes and ages, and all with weary faces. She noticed with curiosity that some of the women now sported curved antlers. Dmitri stepped forward to greet them, and Sybil kept up beside him without making a peep.

"Welcome to the Frost Bridge rest point." He scanned the crowd and seemed to recognize a familiar face. "Trofim, you returned here another year, I see. Did you tell the others what you know?"

A bull that had already shed his horns for the season stepped forward. Despite looking middle-aged, he had not a speck of gray in his fur. "I did."

Dmitri looked out across the crowd with a solemn look. "So, who among you leads the herd? Who journeyed here with your friends, family, and children, knowing there would be no return?"

A larger bull stepped forward now, his horns shedding velvet nearly as much as Dmitri's. "I did. We have come to cross the Frost Bridge. We will not believe your lies any longer, old man."

Dmitri suddenly surged forward and loomed over the bull. Standing side by side with another elk, Sybil could finally see that his large frame and huge antlers were outstanding, even by elk terms. "I have seen dozens more winters than you—yet, you come to challenge my knowledge? I, who journeyed the Frost Bridge to its end? I, who watched as my herd fell from cold, from exhaustion, from starvation? I, who lives my winters out in solace where the cold burns?"

The bull locked horns with him and tried to shake his footing. Sybil nearly leaped forward to help her friend, but Dmitri's footing held. He used his strength to lift the bull by his horns and hurl him to the ground with a single deft swipe. As the bull struggled to stand, a small stream of blood trickling down his face, Sybil decided that Dmitri could handle any scuffle on his own. Besides, a little sparrow like her would end up trampled anyways.

"What's your name, fool?"

"I am no fool," spat the bull. "My name is Artyom. We traveled for miles across Siberia because our souls call out from the other side of the land. You must feel it, too. The path of our ancestors burns in our hearts. We must go to meet them."

"You are fifty winters too late. Each year, the bridge grows shorter and shorter. No elk has returned from the land of our ancestors for as long as I've guarded this place. I offer you food and shelter. I can guide you to the next rest point on your journey south. But I cannot allow you to pass without the knowledge that you will die on the bridge."

A murmur started in the herd as children started to ask questions, but their mothers quickly quieted them. Artyom replied, "If the bridge was closed, we would not hear the call of our ancestors so clearly. They will bless us and allow us passage to their lands, so long as our will does not falter. Ignoring their call leads to starvation. Even you must know that the southern lands offer us little food and too many predators."

"Nonetheless, you must go south or lead your herd to a

drawn-out death." Dmitri slammed down a hoof onto stone with a crash. "Mothers, fathers, will you lead your children to that end? Young bucks, do you desire this end? My job is to ensure your safety. I offer you rest here, free of charge. I will show you where to find food to last until your next rest. The survivors of my herd and of herds like mine dot the coast and will all tell you the same story."

"And yet…" Dmitri paused and nodded his head in reverence to Artyom. "I understand your desires. I, too, fight with my instinct to cross the bridge. Each year, when I feel the need to race forward, I see the faces of my brothers—of my friends. The ones who froze to death at the end of the bridge. The ones who starved and collapsed on our long journey back. You do not have such memories, so I imagine the need must be greater for you. I cannot suppress the instinct given to us by our ancestors, but I can warn you, and I can do what I can to protect you. This is the calling given to me by our ancestors. Please, stay here tonight and give it thought. This home was made for herds to rest in."

"I suppose we must come to an understanding," Artyom replied, reaching out his hand to shake with Dmitri. Dmitri shook it without hesitation, but Sybil saw the glassy look in his eyes. "We will take up your offer and stay here. I extend our thanks to you, but we will also wait to see the herds return. You don't take money, but perhaps we can pay you in goods? We have silks, perfumes, spices, and anything you can dream of wanting."

"I have all the spices and perfumes I need, but a bit of clothing would be nice. I could use a new *chekmen* for myself, and more importantly, I need a winter *chekmen* for my friend here, perhaps a nice sarafan, too. She can no longer migrate and lost all of her belongings on her journey here."

Sybil realized that the expensive clothes that he wore when they first met and the spices for his delicious meals must have been a gift from herds Dmitri helped. He worked so much throughout the year that they grew worn, but new clothing would be easy to come by towards the end of the year. As the herd settled into the rest point, several elk approached her with what appeared to be children's clothing, albeit still resting a little baggy on her legs. The clothes were filled with intricate embroidery that portrayed stories and legends of the elk. Their ancestors, perhaps? The cotton linings kept her so warm that she walked in the twilight and helped the elks without worrying about torpor.

She kept so busy with the herd that by the time night fell and they returned to the half-built building, she still hadn't spoken a word to Dmitri. She had so much to ask, especially about this home they built together, but he seemed nonplussed about the matter. He cooked as he always did despite the silence, though he used ample amounts of turmeric and cumin in today's meal—perhaps he had received a new jar of those spices. As he served the pilaf to her on top of new porcelain plates, he finally broke the silence between them.

"To be honest, it isn't so bad as I said. Those elk will not die on the bridge."

Sybil's mouth gaped. "But you told them they couldn't cross! That the bridge ended before it reached North America. Um, I mean—the land of your ancestors." Avians needed no bridge to reach the Americas, so she was familiar with the flora and fauna that lived there. The reverence that the elk gave it was…strange, to say the least. Perhaps there was something more to those lands than she knew.

"That much is true, but only because the bridge has grown even shorter since the trip my herd made. The herds who do not heed my warning try to return each year, and each year they return earlier than the last. They will reach the end quickly enough, and only the very frail or sick will fall before they return to my lodge and rest. However, the journey south to the next stop is nothing to snuff at, and making it under winter's solstice can lead to starvation, if the ice grows thick enough. I can only supply them with so much before I send them on."

He prodded the fire, and the smoke floated through the

barren frame of the roof. As Sybil watched the trails disappear into the cloudy sky, she saw a white flake glitter and vanish. More of them began to appear and drift closer to their fireplace. She looked outside of the large door to the home and saw the ice building up in small drifts. "Snow…" she whispered. The sight was new and both terrified and excited her.

Dmitri only needed to stand to see out of the house. "Snow indeed. We missed our deadline, but don't worry. I will keep the fire alive for as long as you sleep. The heat will keep us dry, and we will finish the roof in a few days." He sat back down and started to put away his cooking supplies.

Finally, Sybil thought she could respond to his earlier revelation. "I forgive you for lying to me. The elk here also want to migrate, but they can't cross the sea. I also want to migrate, but my wings can't take off." He looked at her strangely, curiosity burning. "Just because I can't go, and just because I am alone, that doesn't mean I have to stop. Like you, I can still help those on their journey. There is always someone needing help."

He nodded. "I'm glad. When we first met, you could barely eat a piroshky. Now, you finish your food and look for more. You want to live again." His smile reached his eyes. "Earlier, I told you I still needed your aid, and that much was true. I am growing old, and many of my friends who survived the journey with me walk ahead of me with our ancestors now. I will leave this place soon, and once I cross that bridge, I cannot help the ones remaining. I was hoping that—"

"You want me to maintain the rest point when you leave," she finished his sentence.

"Yes, I'm hoping for that!" He laughed. "But I don't want you to promise me anything now. This work is difficult, and you must learn to withstand the cold. You need more clothes for that. No, wait until spring to tell me anything. When the air grows warm, you will have all of the clothes and a supply of food to get you to the next rest point. I will send you with a guide to the next rest point, and along with them, a message that your journey be safe and your stay free. Or—"

"Or, I can stay here, in the house we built together. I don't need to wait until spring to tell you that. Maybe I'll go south to get some medicine next year, but I'll return before summer." She sent him a sly wink, and the old man laughed.

"Thank you, but think on it still. The winter is a cruel thing to little sparrows."

She nodded, cleared her plate of pilaf, and asked for the rest.

***

In the next weeks, she helped out as much as she could. One elk was kind enough to fashion valenki boots for her, with spaces for each of her toes and even her hallux. Another gave her a coat made of dyed wool with flowers and vines shaved into the fabric. Despite the number of layers she dressed in, the shortened days and growing cold gradually got under her feathers, until finally she collapsed while scouting for firewood.

She awoke inside of her hut with Dmitri tending to the cobble fireplace. The days became a blur as torpor over took most of her time and the polar nights crept in. She woke to eat and then fell back into a slumber if the fireplace diminished too much. As the wind grew strong, he lined the door with cotton and the walls with clay and tar.

The instinct to migrate south clawed at her. She wanted to step into the cold and fly as far as she could, but each time she thought of it, her feathers shivered and her body froze. Dreams of tropical waters and beautiful song birds and fruit on every tree snuck into her waking hours. Those elk had the same flame burning in them—even Dmitri. Eventually her periods of torpor started to shorten and she grew conscious enough to appreciate his effort.

During one of her rousings, she built up the courage to tell him, "I lost someone important to me, too."

He looked up from the fire in surprise.

"I spent many years with my mate, migrating with him

each winter and spring, and sharing my heart with him. We have our own little nestlings, all wintering in paradise now." She let a smile form on her beak. "He was wonderful, a healer like me, and we flew wherever help was needed. But it couldn't last forever, I suppose."

Dmitri sat back and listened. He could fit in the nest much better now that his antlers had fallen off.

"He became sick. First, he wouldn't stop shivering, and then he couldn't stretch his wings out. We knew no medicine for him, nor did our friends among the healers. I had to watch him suffer all of spring and summer, growing more stiff and lifeless by the day. But he could still..." Tears grew in her eyes. "He could still tell me he loved me until August. That's when he stopped talking. And even then, I could still see it in his eyes. I stayed by his side the whole time. I brought him food and water even as autumn crept in.

"There was no way for him to migrate with me, so I promised him I would not fly until he could. I don't know if that made him happy. He could barely open his eyes anymore. I didn't want to leave him behind. I gave him food for as long as he could eat. I gave him water even when he couldn't open his eyes. And then he spent a week sleeping, as I tried to quench him. A cold wind blew through, and we both went into torpor. When I woke up, he wasn't breathing anymore."

She let silence fill the air as she gathered up the strength for her next part. "I knew I couldn't stay with him. I wrapped him in blankets and used fire to send him to the skies above skies. He flies with the stars now. I started walking south, but when the next cold wind blew, I knew I couldn't make it south. So I went east, through Siberia. I wanted to reach the sea. The sea is always warm." She made a weak laugh. "I thought so, anyways."

"Sometimes I wanted to break my promise and fly south. But when I opened my wings, I would see him staring at me, unable to speak or do anything but look at me sadly. And I couldn't fly again. I stopped trying and focused on walking. I dropped my clothing when my legs grew tired. I dropped my medicine when my legs started to burn. And then I reached here, and I lied to you. I told you I can't fly."

Dmitri sighed. "That's alright. It's the truth, even though a wound had nothing to do with it. When you're as old as me, you've seen the birds with broken wings and the wolves with broken legs. You've seen the elk at the end of the frost bridge who know every direction is death. The birds spread their wings and try anyways. The wolves hunt by sneaking instead of chasing. The elk turn around and walk back, even though they know they will starve. They try to do what they know they cannot. But I have never seen you spread your feathers further than your hands, except when you trip. I know you truly cannot fly."

She laughed, remembering the last time she fell in front of him. He had made fun of the leaves that seemed to be stuck under every feather. "Nothing gets by your eyes, hmm?"

"Nothing!" he affirmed.

"You don't have to tell me to try anymore. In the spring, when it gets warmer and I can go outside in my light clothes again, I will try to fly. I still have so many people to help. I'm sure it's what he would have wanted."

He nodded. "I think so, too. He would want you to eat and to fly. He would want you to make medicines and help anyone you could, wherever you happen to end up."

*****

Every week, he would bring linens, spices, and a bit of the food supply so that she could cook for herself in the hut. The beautiful and foreign designs made her heart brim with gratitude, and she wished she could thank the gift-givers in person. She learned that the few elk that braved the bridge had all returned to them safely. He stacked firewood close to the door in case he couldn't make it to her hut in time to tend the fire, but he never did miss an appointment. Gradually, she became well enough that she grew bored in her time. Eventually she suited up in a full arsenal of cotton and stomped into the snow with frustration. Winter wasn't over, but the days grew longer, and she could help again.

Whenever her shadow grew short, she could shed off a few layers of coats. As the sun grew higher and warmer in the sky, she even forewent her valenki boots and trudged over the snow in bare feet. The elk grew fewer in number towards the end of winter, hopefully all settled in their new southern grounds. Under her heavy cotton clothes, she didn't dare fly, but she at least daydreamed about it. In her visions, she would soar over the lake valley and watch the trees beneath her shrink until they became tiny swatches of color on the wide canvas of the land.

However, as the days became warmer, something started to gnaw at the edges of her mind. Dmitri showed her where all seven stores of food were, and she now helped build them up for when the elk made their return trip. She also helped to clean the lodge, since her familiarity with it took the edge off of her claustrophobia. The visitors grew few and far between until the Frost Bridge rest point seemed lonely. She was glad for the break, but the warmth brought with it something terrifying. Water and lots of it.

When she scouted her favorite peak and looked out towards lake valley, she could see the lake getting deeper and darker. The edge of the glacier wall looked very thin, and a large waterfall cascaded from its edge as melt water filled the lake.

She even brought it to Dmitri's attention. While fluffing the blankets inside the rest point, she did her best to sound calm about the whole thing. "So, Dmitri...do you think that ice will hold up? The waterfall is getting pretty big, and the lake is deeper than it was when I first arrived here."

He flicked a blanket out and made the bed before him. "Oh, that. I have been around plenty enough to know that some ice will never melt. The waterfall will get even bigger than that, and the creek leading out to the sea will grow into a decent-sized river. The bears say fishing gets rather good at the edge of lake valley. Ah, I'll have to introduce you to them.

Nice folks."

Bears? She probably wouldn't ever be ready to meet one bear, let alone a group. What were groups of bears even called? She didn't want to know. She pushed the thought out of her head and pressed on. "Even so, the creek is very close to our lodge. What would happen if a part broke off? If all of the lake fell towards the sea, that little creek couldn't contain it, even if we are next to the ocean."

He shrugged, fluffing a pillow. "You don't have to worry about that. We built your nest high up on the mountain, so the ground around it will stay solid. The river gets close to our lodge, sure, but we're close enough to the ocean that it funnels out nicely. Unless you think the ocean will rise, too?"

"No, I don't think the ocean will rise high enough for that," she replied with exasperation. She rarely stayed in mountains before this, so she had no idea if there was a place that ice couldn't melt. Certainly, Dmitri was wiser than her, but the glacial lake grew deeper with each day, the icy shore shrinking.

Her concentration broke when he threw a pillow at her face. "What was that for?!"

"For worrying over nothing." He took the pillow back and put it in its proper place. "How about this? Let's make a deal. If the glacial river ever does get big enough to reach the lodge—"

"Or the glacier breaks!"

"Yes, or the glacier breaks, then I will stand outside in a place you can see me, and you can fly to get me out of trouble."

She frowned. "I don't think I could fly in time for that. I still have to wear these coats."

"And I don't think the glacier will melt, ever. So do we have a deal?"

She nodded reluctantly. "I suppose."

He ruffled her crest. "Then let's get back to work, shall we?"

***

The weather grew warm enough for her to wear the light sarafan the elk gave her during first snow fall. The glacier had started to creak and mold into strange shapes underneath the weight of the lake. The waterfall grew thick, and the river that cut into the mountainside had even carved through some of the Frost Bridge's ice. Sybil avoided the coast like the plague, while Dmitri scoffed at her wariness and spent all of his time there. The three stores of food above the lake valley became swollen. She started to recognize foods more familiar to her, so filling them became simpler.

On the other hand, the four stores close to the lodge languished. He put up a front, but in the end, travelling too far during the day made Dmitri weary. She sometimes wondered how old he really was and whether he had very many winters left ahead of him. He himself had admitted that he would fly to higher skies soon, but she tried not to think of that. He had his duty here, and she needed to help him with that.

Today, she foraged close to the edge of the lake, searching for berries along the coast. She used a crafted basket to contain them all. She spotted a curled shell slowly moving across stone. A snail! They tasted bland, but she needed protein every once in a while. She couldn't consign herself to the vegetarian lifestyle that Dmitri led. She leaned down to snatch it up in her talons, but a boot quickly crushed it before her.

She yelped and jumped back in surprise. Before her stood a wolf, dressed in thick leather clothing and sporting a crossbow. Her slender frame gave her away as a woman, but that made her no less intimidating. Green fabric circled around parts of her garb so she would blend in with the heath. Sybil opened her wings to fly, but the image of her mate flooded her vision and she froze up before the wolf. Tears flooded into her eyes.

The wolf lowered her crossbow. "Don't start crying. If I wanted you dead, you never would have seen me."

That did nothing to assuage her fear.

"You're Dmitri's little assistant, aren't you? He told us about you."

She nodded meekly. Maybe meeting a bear wouldn't be so

bad after all, if Dmitri was around. Meanwhile, meeting a wolf alone was just a bit too much for her. Her legs started shaking.

"Well, good. I have a message for him. Tell him the glacier is falling today. My pack is moving south until this all blows over. He should move, too, unless he wants to drown in his precious little lodge."

Sybil perked up, but didn't let her guard down. "You think the glacier is melting, too?"

"I know it is."

"If only Dmitri would believe that."

"He is as bull-headed as they come, but today is different. My son hunted at the foot of the waterfall today and saw fish swimming at the bottom of the lake. They were an inch from his own face! He almost poked a hole to see what would happen—that stupid boy—but then he saw the cracks. Tiny little cracks, going all the way across the glacier. They were barely wide enough to see, but they were growing. When I went to see it myself, the cracks were even larger. Instead of blue ice, it is white. It's breaking soon, and I risk myself to leave this message with you."

"Why do you care about him? Aren't you a predator?"

The wolf grimaced, baring her teeth in anger. "We hunt to eat. We do not touch migrators who are in sight of the lodge. The more elk that survive, the more we have to eat in between the rest points. Dmitri helps them survive, and that helps us survive. You help Dmitri, you help us. Consider yourself safe from my pack, but in danger of drowning if you don't move your tail feathers."

She nodded and raced to the edge of the glacier. Even if she couldn't fly, perhaps she could glide. She turned to the wolf to thank her, but saw only empty air. She had already blended back into the forest, perhaps to join her pack and find safety. Sybil also needed to protect her flock.

She looked down at the glacier below her, and sure enough, the ice was filled with huge white cracks. She could see small bubbles moving towards the waterfall under the surface, trapped in an invisible flow. She spread her wings again, preparing to glide away, but as she did she felt cold slush flow over her feet. The ice beneath her was breaking. She flapped backwards to keep from slipping and the ice gave way beneath her in the scramble.

Another waterfall formed, small at first but growing. The waterfall grew deeper quickly as the water pushed ice out in large chunks. Finally, it met with the main waterfall and formed a huge flow. The ice in between the two falls held together, but the glacier itself began to shake. With horror, she watched more falls form on the other side of the glacier's edge. The thin sheet of ice separating the lake from empty air warped, twisted, and finally buckled. The crack of the wall giving way sent a blast of sound straight into her ears and through the waving trees around her.

Just like that, wind flowed under her wings and she was thrust up by the shock wave. She flapped to stay away from the rapids tearing below, unable to escape the flow of wind it pushed forward. Her ears still buzzed from the crack of ice, but she could hear the sound of water flowing louder and louder behind her.

She stopped trying to struggle against the flow of the wind and flapped upwards, looking out towards the sea. The lodge was well within the path of the water, but she didn't see Dmitri anywhere close. She breathed a quiet prayer, hoping he wasn't just below the glacier when it broke. She looked next at the four food stores and finally spotted him next to one. He wasn't close to any kind of clearing and he stood frozen in place. Could he see her? Would he run somewhere she could grab him? He didn't seem like he wanted to move at all.

As the wind pushed her ever closer, she swept forward and low. Instead of thinking of her promise to her mate, she only thought of Dmitri's life. She would have to try and grab him from between the tree branches. Suddenly, his wide eyes locked with hers. "Grab on!" she screamed.

He held his arms up and she wrapped her talons around his

arms. They broke flesh and he gave a yelp, but Sybil could do nothing to temper that pain.

"Hold on tight, this will hurt!"

His fingers grew tight around her ankles as she struggled to lift above the tree line and—more importantly—the height of the water. Her wings were weary from flying for the first time in half a year, but the wind helped her immensely. It pushed her up and forward, towards the sea. For the first minute, she could hear branches smacking him around and more grunts of pain, but she managed to clear the tree line. She couldn't carry Dmitri very far, so she used every ounce of energy from the wind that she could. She soared higher and higher until she thought she could escape the brunt of the water.

She circled south, away from the creek bed, pushing until her wings burned and the wind no longer lifted them up. As they got closer to the land again, Dmitri dropped down and ran beneath her. She tried to land, too, but her momentum sent her into a tumble. He caught up and plucked her off the ground, continuing to run with huge strides. He started huffing as he raced up a mountainside and finally stopped at the frost line. He was panting and wheezing, and Sybil hoped his heart wasn't going to give out. She was exhausted herself and could barely move her wings.

They watched quietly as the water emptied from the valley. The mountain around it gave way and flowed into the sea, and with it her favorite foraging spot. The creek bed grew into a gouge mark that cut into the sea, and the ocean ice buckled from the added water. The glacier cracked apart, tumbling and crashing until the entire Frost Bridge shattered.

Soon enough, the bridge had been carried away entirely. With time, the flow of the rapids finally started to subside. Instead of the cliffs and foothills that hugged the ocean, Sybil saw a huge plain devoid of any trees or plants or signs of life. Instead of a lake, she saw a hollow filled with mud and slush and boulders. Fish flopped desperately to escape, but the mountains were already swallowing the area with mud. She suddenly remembered her hut was on a nearby peak, then sighed with relief as she saw her mountain was nearly untouched—but wait, what about...?

She scanned the coast for any sign of the Frost Bridge rest point, but—just like the Frost Bridge—any traces of it had been swept away. Three of the ground store locations had also been wiped clean, plus one of her mountain stores had been swept away in a mudslide. That left them with just three food stores and a single hut that could barely fit a sparrow and an elk.

Dmitri knelt down, his eyes torn away from the spectacle and burning a hole into the ground instead. "It's gone. It's all gone..." he whispered.

Sybil slowly stepped up to him and wrapped a wing around him. Although he was kneeling, he was still a bit taller than her. She said quietly, "We can gather more food."

"That isn't what I mean!" he shouted, turning on her with a piercing glare. She startled, but held her ground. His expression softened and he looked back out towards the sea. "I'm sorry, I spoke too harshly. I was talking about the Frost Bridge. It's washed away..."

She nodded and followed his gaze at the ocean. "That's a good thing, isn't it?"

A smile slipped across his face. "It is, isn't it? My job is done."

"What do you mean?"

"I lived here for years just to keep people off that damn bridge." She had never heard him swear before. "And now it's gone. There's no way to walk to the land of our ancestors. The bridge will become just a dream—a fairy tale mothers tell their calves. And I will be gone soon, too. It's over. I am glad I got to meet you, Sybil."

She frowned. Something seemed strange about him. "People will still come here. You still have work to do."

He shook his head and said sternly, "No. It's time for me to leave." He stood up, shook the mud off of his clothes, and began to walk away from the sea as if nothing ever tied him there in the first place.

Sybil walked behind him, taking three or four steps to match his stride now.

"Don't follow me."

"But where are you going?" she asked after him. Her eyes were starting to water.

"It doesn't matter. The summer grounds. The land of my ancestors. Away from here."

"But the lodge—" Sybil crashed into his legs as he stopped abruptly.

"The lodge is gone!" He didn't glare at her angrily as he did before, but she could see sadness in his eyes. "Goodbye."

She stood quietly as he walked away. He disappeared into the woods and she let her tears flow.

***

Dmitri crossed into a clearing and allowed himself to finally rest. The long day was nearly over, and his heart ached. He didn't want to leave her so abruptly, but if he didn't, she would probably linger too long next to him. He didn't have much longer to live, so he would spend it walking through the home of his childhood. The lands were full of hungry predators, and he didn't stand a chance without the strength of a herd to protect him, but these were his last days. He could spend them however he wished. Whether that sparrow would rebuild the rest point, join her flock as they returned north, or resume her duties as a healer—all of them were better than lingering around a dying bull.

He had only the clothes on his back. The rest of it had swept away with the flood. He had known something strange was happening with the glacier, but he saw no need to heed it. The Frost Bridge was his lifeline. The rest point was his cage. As he settled into a cold sleep, he wondered how much time he had left. He would go to visit his friends and family soon.

He would wake up in a new rest point—this one much smaller, with only fellow survivors. They would drag him outside, and he would see the Frost Bridge again, and they would say to him, *It's back. The bridge reaches all the way to the land of our ancestors. And you know what time it is!* It was spring, the time of the return. He looked across the ice bridge and saw the faint outline of familiar figures. His little brother, who had starved on the way across. He was just as little as Dmitri remembered. His mother, who had frozen, waiting for the ice to spread across the sea and grant them passage. And there was his father, who had fallen in exhaustion after carrying him so far. They were all smiling, beckoning to him, ready to return and tell him new tales of lands far away.

His dream was interrupted by the smell of a smoke. Without realizing it, a fire had started next to his sleeping form. He peered across the flames and saw a tiny figure.

"Are you waking up?" she called across the flames.

He said nothing.

"It's strange to see an elk on his own. No, an elk should never walk alone. I won't ask you what brings you to a fate like this."

Through the smoke, he smelled the faint scent of baking bread. She was making piroshkies. Somewhere along the way, the sparrow had learned to cook better than him. She rolled out a bun and threw it at him. He caught it instinctively, but set it down beside him instead of eating it. He realized that some of her wing feathers were bent and broken. Had she flown in the night to find him?

"I know this may inconvenience you, but I have a huge problem. You're the only one who can help."

He finally broke his silence. "What happened?"

"It's not about what happened, but what needs to happen," Sybil replied, biting into her own piroshky. "You see, I want to cross the sea, but the way is blocked. I know there are avians that can fly all the way across, but I am not one of them. So, I've decided that I need to build something. Something huge. I will pay you, of course."

"What is it you want to build?" he asked. Maybe she thought the frost bridge would freeze over when winter arrived. In truth, it had been shrinking for some time. Perhaps she had forgotten that.

"Something big. Huge. First, we'll need a rest point, for people like me who can't cross the sea right away. Then we'll build out into the sea, large bridges of wood. That's how they do it in the south seas. Of course, the bridges won't go all the way across, but they will help us build the next thing. Huge ships, big enough to carry a herd."

He frowned. Ships that big simply didn't exist, and there was no way they could cross an ocean.

She seemed unperturbed by this. She finished her piroshky and smiled. "Of course, you don't have to help me with the whole business. In a month, the elks will start to return. You can journey wherever you like, and until then, I will provide you food and shelter. If you want to stay and help me build, you can decide then."

He stared at her. This little sparrow was too weak to lift a log, much less build a rest point or a bridge into the sea. And she wanted to do all that while finding food as well? There was no way for her to do it alone. Her family would return north soon, so he would wait until they arrived, and then depart with the next herd. From there, he would split off and journey on his own. That is, if he lived that long at all. He was old, and probably wouldn't see another winter.

Sybil was smiling at him across the fire, her feet making circles in the snow. She was waiting for him to respond.

"We can talk about payment when the first herd returns. I'll do what I can."

TEMPUS IMPERFECTUM

Al Song

STUTTGART, GERMANY

"No! Stop!" the tall arctic fox shouted as he furiously waved his skinny arms across his chest, signaling the young musicians to put their instruments down. He placed his baton on the stand and took off his bronze wire-rimmed glasses to rub his eyelids. "I know I'm repeating myself when I say this, but you *all* need to practice. It isn't enough that only some of you actually practice. This is a group effort. I will schedule weekend rehearsals if I must."

A chubby badger in the front row with a violin shot a dirty look to the lion next to him. The lion turned towards the badger and gave a nervous shrug.

"We all have to work together, and we need to all be a little more disciplined. It's not fair to everyone if you don't practice or know your part. We're going to be playing music for our town festival. It's our community, so please don't let them down, and especially don't let yourselves down, *alright?*" he said, raising a brow at the last word.

The students groaned an exasperated "okay" together in unison.

The fox looked at his watch, prompting a sigh, and said, "I know it's a few minutes earlier than I usually let you go, but I think we can stop for today. We'll continue next session."

A clamorous commotion of chatting and laughing ensued as most of the students packed up their instruments and sheet music. A few yelled, "See you!" or "Bye, Herr Farber!" as they ran out of the room.

"Herr Farber?" the badger asked, looking up at the lanky fox.

"Yes, what is it, Volker?" the conductor replied as he stashed his baton and sheet music away.

"May Lorenzo and I stay late and practice?" Volker turned to the short otter in thick, black glasses sitting in the front row near him, viola resting on his lap.

The fox's short ears perked, and he smiled at the young badger.

"Of course, but I think some people from the community center have this room booked in half an hour."

"That's fine. We'll be out of here before then."

Lorenzo penciled in a few notes to himself around some dynamics and tempo markings on the score in front of him. He sighed internally as he went back to the first page. The piece was *Waldwelt* by the baroque composer Salvatore Calabrese, and the otter's eyes were fixated on the title, composer, and year of 1601. He tried doing research on Calabrese on the internet without much luck. Lorenzo knew the composer was a brown rat, born on the beautiful beaches of Bari in sunny southern Italy, and composed many short pieces and a couple dozen orchestral works. He was able to find a condensed timeline of the composer's life, but the otter wanted to know how he felt about the world around him besides his affinity for flutes and stringed instruments. Calabrese earned enough to travel to the Holy Roman Empire and kept writing music and performing, but was he happy about his new life? How did he deal with learning a new language? Did he have very many friends and fans when he lived near the Black Forest?

Despite how much Lorenzo enjoyed the music it seemed like Calabrese was a d-list celebrity compared to other composers of his time and wasn't quite as revered, but at least his memory somewhat lived on.

Once the rest of the students and Herr Farber left the room, Volker set his violin down and walked over to Lorenzo. The two grinned at each other in their shared sense of privacy and they embraced with a gentle kiss. The badger's white golf shirt pressed up against the otter's red and yellow t-shirt.

Volker gently pecked him again on the cheek and said, "Why do these people have to be so stressful?"

"Hey, we have time for the whole orchestra to improve," Lorenzo said, letting his Italian accent dictate his palate. "We usually play well at our concerts."

"All the good players graduated. At least you're here."

"*At least?* I've been playing viola since I was eight."

"You know I'm teasing. Let's get back to the music."

The two practiced difficult sections of the pieces to perfect them as much as possible in the dusty music room. Their toes tapped in unison as they ran through the phrases with the precision of a metronome. Their ability to vibrato was unmatched by anyone else in their orchestra. They bowed with such control and pressed the strings their fingerboards with expert precision, their pitch never faltering. Their two instruments were similar in construction and easily mistaken for the other with untrained eyes, yet their sizes and playable ranges differed. The boys always stayed together and listened to one another. They looked and acted very differently, but their common thread was their love for music.

Later on, the afternoon light from the windows turned into a dim golden glow and there was a knock on the door by a middle aged Siberian tigress from the community center. Volker and Lorenzo stopped; it was their cue to leave. They packed up their belongings and ambled out of the school.

The streets of their small town were drenched in a warm shade of honeyed yellow. Trees rustled and shimmered as they reflected soft sunlight from their verdant leaves. Many of the stores and cafes were closed as they walked past their large display windows. A few cars passed by but the late afternoon was fairly quiet.

A couple blocks further down the road of the charming town, the boys passed one of the local bakeries which always stirred up bittersweet memories for Lorenzo.

***

It was a couple years ago, and Lorenzo and his father, Massimo, were still settling into their new apartment in Hügeldorf. The little otter was celebrating his birthday so Lorenzo and his father had a potluck with the other tenants. Helen Themelis was a new Grundschule teacher from Greece. She was a kind rabbit who always helped Lorenzo with his homework and explained to him little things like how to properly format an essay written in German and that quotation marks were written differently. Francisco, a lynx from Spain who studied economics and finance, always helped Massimo with legal paperwork and filing taxes. The Tomruks, a couple of middle-aged Turkish grey wolves who lived next door, would always cook for Lorenzo whenever his dad had to work late. The fellow tenants helped the otters learn German and adjust to living in Hügeldorf.

At the time, Lorenzo had language acquisition classes after school. His father asked him to pick up some bread and gave him a little extra money so he could buy himself a birthday treat. Lorenzo obliged, confident he knew all the terms in German when it came to buying food, purchasing the bread and a little doughnut for himself.

Outside the bakery, the young otter ran into a few other students from the Gymnasium he attended.

"Hey," a bear shouted at him, flanked by a bat and a weasel. "You're the new kid, right?"

Lorenzo took a second to think about what he uttered and nervously replied with, "*Beh*, yeah."

"What are you?" the bear asked smugly.

"I'm an otter," Lorenzo replied quickly.

"No, where're you *from*?" he asked and crossed his arms.

"Italy," the otter answered, clutching the bag of bread tighter.

"Why're you in Germany?"

"My dad needed to find work and—"

"Oh, you're here to steal our jobs, huh?" The bear cut him off. "Why don't you take a hike through the Alps and go back to where you belong?"

It took Lorenzo a moment to string the words together so that they made sense in his mind. "I didn't steal anything."

"You got that bread in your paws. You only got that because we let you live here."

"Please, leave me alone," Lorenzo whimpered.

It was like moving from his small town near Bari to Venice all over again. People picked on him because of where he was from, only now the language barrier was another obstacle. They proceeded to yell things at him and had no idea what the words meant, but inferred that they probably were insults in Swabian.

"It's not as fun when you don't know what we're saying. Learn German already, you stupid foreigner! All you're good for is waiting tables and stealing *our* money."

"Why don't you learn some manners?" a large badger from across the road yelled out at the bullies. The badger stomped towards them, cracking his knuckles and flexing his arms, his scowl housing a fiery ire. Shaking a fist, he shouted obscenities at the bullies until they fled in fear.

The badger turned to the otter and softened his expression. "Are you okay?"

"Yes, I think so," Lorenzo replied, relaxing a bit at the kind face of his rescuer. "Thank you for helping me."

"That's good," the taller boy said with a smile. "Thanks for the help in math class."

"I'm sorry." Guilt seeped into the otter's stomach. This boy saved him and Lorenzo couldn't even recall his name. "What is your name again?"

"I'm Volker." The badger put out a paw.

The otter shook it gratefully. "I'm Lorenzo."

"I remember," Volker said.

Lorenzo felt another pang of guilt. "*Beh*, I'm sorry." He looked to the ground and clutched his groceries.

"It's fine," the badger reassured him. "You're still pretty new here. Those guys are jerks. You don't need to worry about them with me around. Ugh, I can't believe they said those terrible things to you. They say some stupid stuff, but I've never heard them go that far."

"I couldn't understand some of it," Lorenzo admitted.

"Since you helped me with math, I think I can help you with Swabian and teach you some swear words."

***

Despite the hardship of being attacked, Lorenzo smiled at the memory of it because it had brought him close to Volker. It was at that point he gradually stopped spending as much time with his neighbors and started spending more time with his German boyfriend and classmates. Volker introduced the little otter to new friends and people around town, along with showing him the best cafés and restaurants. Through the badger, Lorenzo learned about the different German television shows and how to converse with others their age without sounding like a language textbook.

His father, on the other paw, worked with other Italians and people from around the globe, so Massimo usually spent his free time with his coworkers and their neighbors. It was tough for Lorenzo and his father watching their neighbors gradually leave over the years. After Francisco graduated he went to Frankfurt. The Tomruks moved to Munich to be closer to their children. Helen received a job opportunity at a publishing house in Hamburg. Looking back Lorenzo regretted not spending more time with them before they left.

"Lorenzo?"

"Yeah, Volker?"

"You've been looking kind of sad today and you've been dragging your tail. Is something wrong?" Volker turned to Lorenzo, who stopped in his tracks.

"Um, no," the little otter said and rubbed his arm.

"I know I've been a pain today. I'm sorry if I said something that hurt your feelings."

"No, you didn't say anything wrong."

"Well, I know I've been kind of a jerk lately. The orchestra is hopeless and my parents gave me that talk again about how music is a useless career path."

"I'm sorry about all that." Lorenzo gave his boyfriend a sympathetic look. He wished he could help with all of Volker's problems too, since Volker was his dutiful defender.

"Why do they always have to tell me that music is pointless?" Volker asked, putting down his violin case so he could punch a lamppost. "Why can't they just let me go to a music school? They have money and they both work in finance. Orchestra club is fun, and getting private lessons from Herr Farber is great, but I want to play more. I love music and no one sees that. You're so lucky."

"What do you mean by that?" Lorenzo cocked his head and shrank a little.

"You want to study math and become a math teacher, and your dad supports that." Volker picked up his violin case and started to walk again.

"Maybe if you said you wanted to become a music teacher or something else in the music industry then your parents might be okay with that?" Lorenzo suggested with a shrug.

"But I don't want to teach. You know I don't have any patience for other people, especially children." The badger grimaced, halting in place. Shaking his head, he continued, "We got off track, so what's wrong?"

125

"Nothing," Lorenzo said meekly. "I'm fine. Really, I am. We're close to my place too." He motioned to a gray apartment complex. There were Turkish and Greek flags taped to some of the windows. The largest flag was an Italian one tied to a balcony highlighted by the radiance of the afternoon.

"Hey, I wanted to say I'm sorry again. I know I'm a jerk sometimes."

"Well, you are sweet when you're not angry at the rest of the world."

"I love ya," Volker said as he stroked the whiskers on Lorenzo's face with his thumb and kissed him on the nose. "I'll see you at school tomorrow. Bye." He waved and hurried off.

"*Ciao*," Lorenzo replied with a gentle smile. Lorenzo drew a breath as he looked up at the Italian flag hanging off of the balcony of his apartment, the amber sunlight slowly diminishing behind it as the sky took on hues of red.

***

The next Saturday morning Lorenzo carried his viola with him as he walked to Volker's house. He checked his watch. It was five minutes before nine as he reached the driveway to the house, a one-story abode that was larger than most of the others on the street. He knocked on the door and Volker's mother answered. The tall, slender badger wore a pair of sweatpants along with a worn sweater and was holding a pile of towels. She gave a surprised look and said, "Oh, Lorenzo, Volker's still asleep."

"Yesterday he invited me over for breakfast. I hope he told you, unlike last time," the otter said, frowning at the thought.

"He informed us," she reassured him.

"He said that I should come over at nine."

"Oh, you know Volker. He loves to sleep in," she said and shook her head.

"I guess that's true."

"Come in. I apologize for his rudeness." She stepped aside to let Lorenzo in.

"I think I'm used to his antics by now."

"Well, Herr Farber called last week and said that Volker yelled at other students when they weren't playing correctly, is that true?" she asked, her voice filled with concern.

"Has he called you about that problem before?" he asked, trying to sound playful.

"Yes," she exhaled tiredly. "I swear someone's going to get upset about his temper and it'll be someone bigger than him."

Lorenzo's voice rose in pitch. "He's always been passionate."

"That's one way to describe him." The tall badger sighed. "Lately he comes home from school and he just wants to argue. Apparently asking him to consider a stable career field warrants an endless argument. The orchestra is just an afterschool activity. I loved gymnastics as a cub, but I knew I'd never become a professional athlete."

"He really cares about music. Maybe one day he'll teach classes." The otter's voice wavered.

"If only he had your ability to plan things out. You're going to make a wonderful math teacher one day." The badger beamed toward him.

Lorenzo started fidgeting his fingers. "Yeah, thank you, uh, that's kind of you to say."

They walked down the hallway to Volker's bedroom. The door had a framed picture of Volker in a tuxedo holding his violin and bow. Lorenzo loved how proud Volker looked in it. Lorenzo had the same one on his bedroom nightstand.

"Volker!" she yelled through the door.

"What!?" he yelled back.

"Lorenzo is here!" she belted.

"Okay," he replied in a softer tone with a whiny hint of drowsiness.

Volker was in a faded green t-shirt and white shorts when he opened the door. His fur was bedraggled and his clothes were completely covered in wrinkles. He rubbed his eyes. "Let me get ready first, okay?"

"Alright," Lorenzo replied.

The stocky badger grabbed a towel and ran towards the bathroom.

"I apologize again," Volker's mother said with another sigh. "You can start eating before him. The rest of us had breakfast already."

"Thank you very much, Frau Fiedler, but I'll wait for him."

Lorenzo walked into the living room where Volker's younger brother was watching television. He looked similar to Volker but was shorter and had a lip piercing. Volker's father sat in an arm chair reading the news on his tablet. He wore a red dress shirt, a mustard tie, and black slacks.

"Morning, Lorenzo," Volker's father said without looking up from his device.

"Good morning," Lorenzo replied. "You're all dressed up."

"We're heading to Tübingen to visit my sister today. I'm still waiting for Laura to finish getting ready."

"Tübingen's a pretty town," Lorenzo said with a smile.

"Yep." Volker's father nodded without looking away from the tablet.

Lorenzo looked over at the younger badger. He was dressed in black jeans with frayed holes along the knees and had on a black t-shirt with a British metal band on it. "How are you doing, Fritz?"

"I'm watching TV," Fritz replied curtly.

"Don't be rude, Fritz," his father scolded.

"I'm doing fine and I'm still watching TV," Fritz groaned the statement like a complaint.

"What are you watching?" Lorenzo asked, trying to keep polite conversation between them.

The young badger sighed. "Something."

"Fritz!" his dad scolded.

"*Teen Krimis*," he replied exasperatedly.

On the wall-mounted television was some program about teenagers solving crimes and having good old fashion adolescent drama, which actually meant problems fabricated by adults who thought they knew what teens were going through in the modern day. It was a little schmaltzy for Lorenzo, but it did manage to make him laugh at times. Usually the laughs were directed at the show rather than its jokes, though.

Why did the criminal have to be Turkish? Why did the comic relief sidekick, who was portrayed as someone not very bright, have to be the guy with a badly executed Italian accent? Why was there only one girl in the main cast? These problems bewildered Lorenzo since it was the twenty-first century, but then again, the battle against unfair representations was still ongoing.

He remembered turning on the television set when he first got into Germany and not understanding anything, so the internet felt like a sanctuary for him. He could read comics and watch Italian television on his laptop. As his German skills developed he was able to watch television and read German newspapers and magazines. Lorenzo realized that he was reading significantly less in Italian, while his father mostly read Italian novels he ordered online.

Volker's mother returned, now wearing a yellow summer dress with green leaves sprinkled on it. She quickly began packing various things in a small suitcase for their trip, transferring her belongings from one tote bag with a beach theme on it to another with a forest scene printed on it.

Lorenzo smiled at the feeling of being around this badger family. They were all off doing different things but he was surrounded by sounds and life. He was around people who accepted him, and he didn't feel awkward being in this space.

After another couple of minutes, Volker walked into the living room wearing a pair of jeans and a golf shirt. He gave a yawn and said, "Alright, let's eat."

The table was covered in bread and a couple spreads. The bread slicer was parked on the counter still covered in crumbs. Lorenzo grabbed a piece of toast and spread some yogurt cream on it. He licked his lips at the sight of it and felt relief as he took a bite.

"Oh, I almost forgot, my dad said he wanted to have lunch

with both of us in Stuttgart today. Do you want to come along?" Lorenzo asked after his first couple bites.

"Yeah, of course. Is it the same restaurant?" Volker asked as he spread some cheese onto his toast.

"Yep."

"Cool, I love that place!" Volker grinned. His mother walked into the room as she threaded earrings through her perked up ears. He turned to her and asked, "Mom, can I go to Stuttgart today with Lorenzo? His dad wants to have lunch."

"I don't see why not." She shuffled through her purse and took out two twenty euro bills. "Here, have fun."

"Thanks, Mom," Volker said with a cheesy smile.

Lorenzo just gave him a look that read, *I thought I was the one with a brown muzzle.*

Volker shot a defensive look back. "What?"

"Nothing," the otter replied, shaking his head.

When they finished eating they got their instruments out and started to practice difficult sections in the pieces again. A couple minutes into the practice session Volker's mom told him that they were leaving and that Fritz was going over to his friend's house.

At around half past eleven, they finished practicing and walked to the train station. After buying their passes from the old, rusted ticket machines, they bought some candy from a kiosk and waited for their train, sharing some Turkish delights and Polish chocolate covered marshmallows.

Once their train arrived, they sat down in a section of empty seats and looked out at the quaint scenery. All the brick buildings, lush hills, and flourishing trees rushed by them as they headed towards the city.

Upon reaching their destination, they left the train and walked up an escalator. The bright sun welcomed them out of the underground station to a busy street filled with shoppers and couples. There were tourists taking pictures and people avoiding the photographers. The two ambled towards Schloss Platz and then down a pedestrian street with stores and restaurants.

They entered a clothing store with an abundant amount of sales, promotions, and signage. Walking into the men's section, Volker noticed a t-shirt with *Voglio una bella ragazza* on it. "Look, it's in Italian," he said as he plucked it off of the rack. The shirt was a garish mess of sparkles with cacographic lines and colors scrawled on it.

"That says, 'I want a pretty girlfriend' and it's kind of gaudy," Lorenzo replied.

"Alright, I'll put it back," he said with a playful tone of defeat.

"Why is everything in English, Italian, and French? Shouldn't some of these clothes be in German?"

"Having things in other languages is cool," Volker said as he picked up a t-shirt with *C'est la vie* in a typeface emulating graffiti on it.

They looked around a little more. Lorenzo tried on some button-ups and a few scarves while Volker tried a couple hoodies on. Volker finally decided on an olive green colored jacket, a scarlet t-shirt, and some plain white socks. He went up to the counter with a buck behind it. The cashier had on all of the latest trendy clothing including ripped denim, a trucker hat with indents on the sides for his antlers and a gaudy gold chain around his neck. Volker took out the money his mom gave him and some of his own and paid for the clothes.

They left the store and walked to a small gelato shop nearby that was built into the façade of a shopping center. A kangaroo received his cup of gelato and skipped away past the two as they approached the counter.

A young red vixen and a large black bear stood in the small space behind the display of gelato speaking in Italian together. They wore white aprons on top of their casual clothing, and had green and red visors on.

"A scoop of strawberry, pistachio, and vanilla, please," Volker said and placed a few euros on the counter. The bear scooped the three flavors of gelato into a cup and gently placed a spoon in it for the badger.

"I'd like *Tiramisu, Amarena,* and *Zabaione* please," Lorenzo said with a smile.

"Are you from Italy too?" the vixen asked the otter switching to Italian.

"Yes, I'm from a town near Bari. Are you from Rome?" Lorenzo guessed from her accent.

"Yep, and so is my boss," she said as she tilted her muzzle towards the bear. "I came here to study German history and I was lucky enough to find a job here." She handed him the cup of gelato.

Lorenzo thanked her. "*Grazie mille.*"

"*Di niente,*" she replied.

"You ready?" Volker asked the otter.

Lorenzo grabbed a napkin and replied with "*Si, andiamo.* Oh, I mean, yeah, let's go."

They walked back toward Schloss Platz. They passed a couple people with "Free Hugs" signs in English and they both gave a handsome wolf a hug. They watched a ferret and fox couple playing guitars. A cardboard sign propped in front of the guitarists read, "Need money for train fare to Vienna."

Schloss Platz was the largest square in Stuttgart and was surrounded by large shopping centers, museums, and a baroque castle. The pillar in the center had a statue of a fox with feathered angel wings along with wolf figures near the bottom of spire. The two fountains flanking the pillar had sculptures of various species under the spouts of water. The statues were weathered into a jade green tone from time and the elements.

"The fountain on the left or the right?" Volker asked.

"The one on the right," Lorenzo replied.

They sat down on the edge of the fountain and Lorenzo took off his white sneakers. The otter pulled his khakis up a bit and put both of his feet in the water. He happily kicked and splashed the water towards the center of the fountain. Volker sat facing away from the fountain and looked at the crowds of people. A couple of foxes were flying kites and many people had towels out and were relaxing under the warm sun. Another otter watched over her three cubs, who were playing in the fountain.

The two fed each other gelato and made small talk. A few clouds drifted above the pair as they felt a slight chill in the atmosphere. Spring flowers bloomed and some of the people shed their clothes and fur.

Lorenzo looked at his cup of gelato. The logo had an Italian flag crossed with a German one. It read, "Gelato Freddo."

Volker turned to him and said, "There it is again. Why are you sad? Is it the gelato? Is it because I woke up late?"

Lorenzo realized that he was frowning at the cup's logo and tiredly replied, "Volker, I just don't want to talk about it." He finished his last bite and put the cup down behind him on the grass.

"Why can't you just tell me what's wrong?" Volker asked in a calm tone.

Lorenzo remained silent and stared at the water.

"You can tell me anything. You know that," he continued with an understanding voice.

"Okay." Lorenzo released a big sigh and kept staring at the water. "Last week, I went to a deli to buy some cheese for my dad's new recipe. There was an Italian fox who needed help because he didn't speak German. So I assisted him with directions and translated things for him, and then we talked about Italy. There was an old person outside who yelled, 'Go back to your own country! Why can't you foreigners learn to speak German?' The fox had no idea what he said, and he kept speaking to me in Italian, and the elderly guy kept yelling mean things at us. I didn't explain what he was saying because I didn't want him to feel bad too. So I just said that the old guy was spouting nonsense."

"I'm sorry about that," Volker said, giving Lorenzo a hug and kiss.

"You don't have to be sorry, you didn't do anything wrong."

A couple of teenagers around their age noticed that they

had kissed and walked up to them. A stout squirrel about as tall as Volker asked in a smarmy tone, "So which one's the girl?"

The rest of the small group laughed.

Volker balled his paws into fists and stood up. Lorenzo tensed up and he turned his gaze back at the water. His whiskers faltered.

The mother otter turned away from her cubs playing in the fountain and yelled, "Leave them alone! They're not bothering you!"

The squirrel and his associates backed off and walked away, remaining loud and obnoxious.

"Thanks for that," Volker kindly said. He turned to Lorenzo who looked like he was going to cry.

"It's no problem," said the mother otter. "I have to teach my children that prejudice is wrong."

Volker checked the time on his phone. "Maybe we should leave. We don't want to be late for lunch." He helped Lorenzo up and the two disposed of their cups. Volker picked up his shopping bag and they started to walk in the direction of the restaurant.

There were smaller boutique stores in the streets with less foot traffic. They passed cute stores and people wearing black sunglasses and incredibly fashionable, yet expensive looking clothing. The sun was still happily beaming at the world but as they walked Lorenzo was frowning the entire time.

"Is it about those jerks?" Volker asked.

"Yeah," the otter replied.

"But that lady stood up for us, isn't that what's important?"

"But those guys still harassed us." Lorenzo sighed.

"Doesn't it make you feel good that other people actually defended us?"

Lorenzo sighed again. "I guess a little."

Volker countered with a smile. "Let's just have lunch and forget about it, okay?"

"Alright," the otter replied. He tried to put on a small smirk, but it quickly faded.

Lorenzo's father told him when they first moved to Baden-Württemberg that the restaurant was a cross between a traditional pizzeria and a döner shop. The owner was an Italian hyena who fell in love with a Turkish fennec fox. They opened the restaurant together and it became successful. The building itself was aged but the business was relatively new. The windows and signage were free of cracks and smudges, and the interior decor didn't look worn and weathered like most of the other older businesses around the area.

When they arrived, Lorenzo's father, Massimo, greeted them with a big wave from a seat on the outside of the restaurant. "Lorenzo! Volker!" he shouted. *"Ah, mio figlio e il suo ragazzo. Come stai, Lorenzo?"*

"I'm okay," the short otter grumbled.

Volker turned to his boyfriend. "Wait, what did he say?"

"He just asked how I was doing," Lorenzo explained.

"E tu?" the large otter asked Volker.

"That means 'And you?' right?" Volker inquired.

Lorenzo sighed. "Yeah."

"Oh, uh, good," the badger answered.

"Dad, can we just stick to German?" Lorenzo groaned. "I mean, for Volker's sake."

Massimo nodded. "Alright, sure thing."

The two of them sat down. The patio was crowded; all of the other seats outside were taken. There was a table with a wolf family speaking in Greek and another table with a couple of teenage goats speaking Turkish and laughing. Other people could be heard speaking in Vietnamese and French at the other tables.

"Alright, in German, how's your day been?" Massimo asked.

"I'm fine," Lorenzo wearily replied. "I thought I already said that."

"Yeah, we had a great time in the city," Volker said, trying to liven up the mood. "We went shopping and we had gelato."

"That sounds delightful," Massimo said.

An older tiger waiter walked out with a big grin on his face.

"*Massimo, come stai?*" He and Massimo gave each other a big hug and kissed one another on the cheeks.

"What did he say?" Volker asked Lorenzo.

"He just asked how my dad was," the short otter said glumly.

"Oh yeah," Volker said with a nervous chuckle.

"It's okay," Lorenzo replied with a frown. He stared down at the menu while the waiter and his father talked.

"What's wrong now, Lorenzo?" Volker asked.

"Nothing," the little otter said, feeling upset at everything.

When Massimo and the waiter finished talking, the three of them ordered. A while later the waiter came back with their pizzas and drinks. He placed a carafe of orange juice down and set a bottle of Apfelschorle and Sprudel next to it before distributing the pizzas. Lorenzo had ordered his favorite falafel pizza with tzatziki sauce and feta. Volker got a Margherita pizza, and for Massimo, one topped with figs, cashews, and various traditional Turkish spices.

Lorenzo took a bite of pizza and smiled. He noticed that Volker was looking back at him and smiling at his countenance.

"Feeling any better?" Volker asked him.

"I guess," he looked up with a slight grin.

"Lorenzo, was there something wrong earlier?" his father asked him.

"No, everything's fine," Lorenzo replied meekly and his joyous grin faltered.

"Lorenzo, if there's something wrong you can tell me."

"No, really, everything's great," he blurted quickly and turned his gaze toward his slice of pizza, timidly taking another bite.

"Alright, if you say so," the older otter said. He then turned to Volker. "What's new with you, Volker?"

"Besides the idiots in the orchestra, I've been pretty good." The badger scowled, but covered it up with another bite of the pizza. "Thanks for lunch by the way," he said between bites.

"You're welcome. I'm sure that you will all do fine. I know

you and Lorenzo have been practicing a lot and that will help the rest of the group."

"Yeah, Lorenzo's perfect at the viola," Volker said, smiling at his boyfriend, "and he himself is perfect."

"Aw, that's sweet. Young love," Massimo said as he tilted his head and grinned at the two.

Lorenzo looked down at his pizza again and blushed under his whiskers. "You could have said that in Italian, Dad."

"*Oh, mi dispiace, Lorenzo.*"

"What's that mean?" Volker asked.

"He apologized. You can go back to speaking German now," Lorenzo ordered.

Massimo rolled his eyes. "The orange juice please, my sir."

Lorenzo pushed it despondently towards his father. Massimo grabbed the carafe, knocking over Lorenzo's glass of Sprudel. It splashed on him and soaked his white shirt and khakis.

"Be careful, Dad!" he yelled.

"*Mi dispiace!*" Massimo tried to help but his napkin was already dirty. He reached into his backpack for a rag but accidentally knocked it over on its side as well. A couple miscellaneous items spilled out. A young mink was walking by and a pen rolled against her crimson high heel. Massimo called out to her, "*Signorina, aiutarmi perfavore!*"

Volker handed Lorenzo an unused napkin and asked, "What is he saying now?"

"He asked her for help," the smaller otter said through gritted teeth as he patted himself down. "Dad, she doesn't speak Italian!" Lorenzo shouted at his father.

"*Beh, ma—*" his father sputtered, defeated.

"Just speak German!"

"Lorenzo, come on, don't yell at your dad like that," Volker said putting a paw on his boyfriend's shoulder.

All of the other customers including the mink were staring at Lorenzo.

"I think that I'm done here," Massimo said calmly with a

forced smile. "It's good to see you again, Volker."

"Is there a problem?" the waiter asked as he walked back outside to see what was happening.

"No, we had a spill. May we have the bill now?" Massimo answered.

Massimo quickly paid for the pizzas and left with a subdued, "Goodbye."

Lorenzo and Volker finished their meals in silence before heading home, Lorenzo's stomach left queasy from the entire ordeal.

***

On the way back, Lorenzo stayed quiet as a cloud of gloom surrounded him. During the train ride, he stared out at the indifferent world rushing past him. Volker tried to console him, but the otter uttered only one word responses.

At Lorenzo's apartment, the two teens sat on the lumpy corduroy couch and watched television. Lorenzo stared into the colorful box, his ears drooping, but wasn't paying attention to anything. He leaned against Volker, who stared down at his boyfriend and rubbed his side.

"Are you feeling any better now?" Volker asked.

Lorenzo took a second to think about the next words that would exit his mouth and replied, "No, I'm still feeling guilty." He took a deep, sharp breath. "I'm still upset at those guys that were making fun of us and that old person who was yelling at me."

"Does it matter though? I mean, I guess it does, but we don't have to deal with them anymore, and we don't have to listen to them."

"It's not going to be the last time though," Lorenzo said.

"Shouldn't things like this make us stronger?"

"I don't feel like it's making me any stronger." The otter sighed and then let out a groan of frustration. "I'm tired of people harassing me."

"I know people aren't the most open-minded here in the rural world, but at least we're not being killed on the streets or jailed for just being ourselves, right?"

"Even though I'm not dead or in prison, it's still not okay and it still hurts."

"I know it does." Volker held his boyfriend.

Lorenzo leaned into the badger and closed his eyes. "Ever since I was little, I never felt like I really fit in or like I was actually a part of a group." He took a breath and sat back up. "When I moved from southern Italy to Venice I didn't have a lot of friends and some of the other kids would make fun of me because of my dialect. They made it seem as if I was a stupid or lazy person because of how I spoke and where I came from." He looked at the speckled carpet. "Back then, I wasn't sure if I had any real friends. When we moved here I had to learn a whole new language. Other people would make fun of me because I was still learning how to speak German, and even now people still make fun of me because I have an accent. There were also the people who harassed me because I'm a foreigner. Today I just wanted to have my dad speak German because it would make us seem less foreign."

Volker gently rubbed Lorenzo's back. "It's not like people can look at you and be able to tell that you're not German."

"I know that, but when I speak I sound different. After they hear me, people know that I'm a foreigner." Lorenzo stared at the ground again.

"You don't sound funny. I think your accent is *molto* sexy," Volker said, giving Lorenzo a playful look.

Lorenzo gave a small chuckle but sighed again. "But that's the thing. I have an accent and that makes me different."

"We're gay, that already makes us different. Everyone's different."

"I know, but it's not like being gay makes it any easier. I'm glad I'm gay since you're my boyfriend," he said and squeezed the badger's bicep. "You're so big and strong."

"Aw, cutie," Volker said, giving Lorenzo a small kiss on his furred cheek. "Does it matter what people think?"

"I care about what you think."

"Well, I'm not just anyone. I'm your friend and your boyfriend. And Lorenzo, you shouldn't yell at your dad like that," the badger said gently.

"I know."

"Seeing you shout at your dad was kind of surprising. I've never seen you get angry at him or anyone. I mean, my parents get on my nerves a lot but I don't yell at them, at least not like that," Volker said as he tried to make the last part sound like a joke.

Lorenzo looked even more ashamed and turned his head away.

Volker rubbed his back again. "I'm not trying to tell you that you're a bad person for yelling at him, but it just didn't seem fair or okay."

"I guess I could have just politely told him."

"Or you could have just told him the truth about what was going on." The badger gave the otter a reassuring look and a hug.

"Yeah, I didn't want to make a scene by worrying him, but I ended up making one anyways. I really wish that having an accent or being from a different country wasn't a big deal."

"Even people here think that if you have a thick regional accent or if you have trouble with Hochdeutsch then you're uneducated," Volker said, shaking his head.

"I guess I sometimes feel as if I'm in a country that doesn't really want me to be here. I know that immigration is a big deal in many countries. It seems like even in Italy there are people who aren't fond of immigrants."

"Really?" Volker asked, surprised at the notion.

"I guess people who emigrate from Africa or the Middle East into Italy also have to deal with discrimination," Lorenzo said glumly.

"It's terrible. I mean, I know there are still some people that dislike immigrants but not all people are xenophobic."

"I know that, but sometimes I really wish that I weren't so different."

"Like I said, we're all different," Volker said with reassurance.

"Yeah but I wish I didn't have to feel this way. It's not enough that I'm gay, but I'm also an immigrant."

"You don't have to keep thinking about this all the time. I try to just let it go and forget about it," Volker said.

"Maybe you're just tougher than me."

"It doesn't mean that it still doesn't hurt when people say homophobic things." The badger frowned.

"I'm sorry. I didn't mean it like that," Lorenzo said quickly and looked back at the ground.

"It's okay. I know that people are afraid of me. I know that they think I'm gonna beat them up. I still remember the day I met you. We were sitting next to each other in math class and I knew you were a little scared of me being this big, angry guy. But when I was having trouble with some of the math problems, you helped me with everything, and you were so patient with me." Volker kissed Lorenzo on his forehead.

"I was afraid of coming out to you. I was scared that you wouldn't want to be my friend anymore. Plus I had a crush on you after you saved me from those xenophobes."

"I was afraid too. I knew a lot of people already didn't like me but when you came out to me you gave me the courage to do it too."

Lorenzo blushed. "Aw, Volker."

"We're out of the closet. We shouldn't care about people's stupid opinions. We have friends with families that moved here from other countries too, like Turkey, Greece, and Poland. You're not alone, Lorenzo. You've got friends and me. You also have your dad."

Lorenzo smiled at the thought and Volker gave him a tight hug. "I love you, Volker."

"I love you too, Lorenzo."

The two of them cuddled and watched television until Lorenzo's father returned home a few hours later.

"I see you two have been having fun," Massimo chided with a small grin on his face.

"I was just about to leave. Oh yeah, I still have your viola at my house," the badger said quickly. "I'll bring it back to you tomorrow."

"Okay, thanks," Lorenzo said with his paws in his lap and his head down.

"See you, Lorenzo," Volker said, blowing his boyfriend a kiss.

Lorenzo caught it and gave a little wave.

"Goodbye, Herr Agresta," Volker said to Lorenzo's dad.

"Bye, Volker," Massimo said kindly in his low voice.

The badger took his shopping bags and left the apartment.

Lorenzo's father put his belongings away in his room and walked back out. The large otter plopped beside his son on the couch and asked, "Can we speak in Italian now?"

"Of course we can," the smaller otter said, his head still bowed and the feelings of guilt resurfacing.

"What was all of that about earlier today, Lorenzo?" Massimo said as Lorenzo felt a large paw rest gently on his shoulder.

"I'm sorry, Dad. I feel really awful about that," he whimpered. He put his glasses on the side table, placed his head on his father's chest, and hugged him.

His father rubbed his back and patted him on the head.

"I'm really sorry for yelling at you," Lorenzo said. He sat up and wiped the forming tears from his eyes. "Some stuff happened today and some other stuff happened last week."

"What happened?" Massimo asked him calmly. He hugged the little otter tighter. "You can tell me anything that's been going on."

Lorenzo recounted the incident with the Italian tourist at the deli. Massimo nodded and listened quietly with understanding eyes.

"And what happened today?" Massimo asked gently.

"Some guys were harassing Volker and me because we were

kissing."

"Did they hurt you?" Massimo's voice filled with concern.

"No, they didn't hurt us and there were some adults there who told them to leave us alone."

"So you've been sad because someone told you those things and because some boys were making fun of you?"

"It hurts, dad." Lorenzo sobbed. His large tail slumped against the couch.

"I know it hurts. People are terrible to me too."

"I just don't want to tell you things because I don't want to worry you."

"I'd rather have you tell me what's wrong than you shouting at me."

"Dad, you have enough to take care of and I don't want to be a burden."

"Lorenzo, if you have an issue then I want you to come to me and tell me. I want you to know that I'm someone you can trust. I'm your father. I know you're grown up and you want to keep things to yourself, but I want to help you."

The shorter otter took a breath. "Alright."

"I remember that you didn't even tell me that your uncle Armando used to hit you until we moved out. I was so angry at him. I called him and yelled at him. I don't think we'll ever be able to go back to Venice after that. He was so rude and angry. He tried so hard not to seem like a 'southern Italian' yet he was so pompous and acted like he was so much better than me."

Lorenzo looked at the ground at the mention of his uncle. "I was afraid that he'd hurt me more if I told you."

Massimo hugged his son tightly. "He's horrid. I would never hit you, and I don't understand why he would ever do that to you. I don't think any parent should hit their child. Children don't deserve that."

"I hated being in Venice. I hated how the other children would make fun of me because of our accent and the fact that we were from the south. I would always do better than them at tests, and they would still always call me stupid. When we lived near Bari, I didn't have to worry about other people making fun of me."

"I knew you were angry with me for leaving Pietre dei Marini and then again for leaving Italy, but I knew that this would be good for us. Things are better now," Massimo said with relief in his voice. "We don't have to live with my idiotic brother, and I don't have to depend on him. I have my own money and I'm happy. When we were in Venice I couldn't find a job that would pay me well enough to give us a chance to live alone."

"I guess some things are better. I'd rather be living here than with Uncle Armando."

"You know, when your mother divorced me I was so afraid, and I didn't know what to do. Grandpa and grandma had passed away a year before so I couldn't turn to them. You always made me so happy, and I felt like I had to do everything in my power to protect you. When I lost my job and I couldn't afford our home and we had to move in with that idiot, I felt like a failure. When I lost my job again in Venice, it felt even worse."

"I'm sorry you had to go through that." Lorenzo knew the story already but wanted to console his father.

"But you were there with me. You've always been with me. I know that we don't have much but what we do have is ours, I'm happy living in Germany with my son. I love you so much, Lorenzo."

"I love you too, Dad." The little otter looked up at his father with so much pride and gratitude in his heart.

***

The evening of the spring festival turned the small, quiet town of Hügeldorf into a sparkling party. The buildings and trees were covered in lights, and lanterns hung across lampposts. Food vendors lined the main streets, and people cheered and talked to one another. Neighbors reacquainted themselves, and children ran around with food and sweets.

There was a makeshift stage in the middle of the town square where the Gymnasium orchestra played. The orchestra was made of diverse students of different species and class grades sitting in their different instrument's sections performing together to create beautiful music in unison.

Herr Farber pierced the air with his baton at the last note of the piece. His face, which was starting to change to its summer coat, looked overjoyed at the performance of the students. There was a huge cheer from the audience, and they all applauded with ferocious enthusiasm.

Both Lorenzo and Volker looked across to one another in the front row and smiled. In the crowd Lorenzo's father and Volker's family sat next to each other. Volker's mother recorded the performance with a camcorder. Volker's brother and father weren't paying attention, instead they were on their tablets, distracted by television and the news.

Herr Farber gestured for the students to stand and they bowed to the audience. Everyone could tell that arctic fox was proud of the young musicians. The audience demanded an encore but the next musical act was up.

Volker and Lorenzo left the stage with their instruments in tow as a smaller jazz band started to set up. It looked like it consisted of older members of the community. Herr Farber remained on the stage as he was also their conductor. The two gave a small wave at the arctic fox from off of the stage and he waved back.

"Volker, do you think we can go by the fountain?" Lorenzo asked. "My feet are kind of hot."

"Of course we can. Let's give our stuff to our parents first so we don't have to carry it around," Volker suggested.

They received hugs from Volker's mom and Lorenzo's dad and left their belongings with them. The two walked down a small road illuminated by glowing streetlamps and stringed lights. They held each other's paws after they scouted the area to make sure no one else was around. A little while later they reached a small rectangular fountain that wasn't running.

Lorenzo hurriedly took off his dress shoes and socks. He pulled the legs of his tuxedo pants up and dipped his feet in the cold water with a relieved sigh. Volker just sat on the edge of the fountain facing away from the water.

"I do miss being near the sea," Lorenzo said as he splashed around a little bit. The jazz band played a fast-paced swing piece in the background and Volker swayed to the music. "When I lived near Bari we were on the coast. I would go swimming with my dad and my friends all the time."

Lorenzo looked at the dark shops around them. One of the stores sold art supplies and had a painting of the Alps in the front window. To his left was a floral shop that had a sale on small potted trees. He sighed and said, "The hills and the forest are beautiful here, but I still wish it wasn't landlocked."

"Yeah, the ocean is beautiful, but at least there are rivers. I thought you liked hiking through the Black Forest with me."

"I do, but I still like swimming a lot more. There's just something about being surrounded by water that puts me at ease."

"I guess I really like beach vacations in the north and the ones in France. I'm not a fan of the rocky beaches in Marseilles though. Hopefully one day I can go to Italy with you and see the beaches there," Volker said and smiled at the otter.

"I don't plan on going back anytime soon though," Lorenzo said gently kicking the water with a sigh. He thought about his time at the restaurant with Volker and his father. The awareness of how disconnected he was with Italian culture pained him while still feeling as if it was his own fault.

"Maybe we could travel together somewhere one day," Volker said.

"You seem happier this week… or at least less angry at people."

"Oh, thanks," the badger said sarcastically.

"I didn't mean any offense by it," the otter said.

"I know, I'm just joking with you. We played well for today."

"We played *well?*" Lorenzo said incredulously. "It was amazing!"

"It could have been better," Volker replied.

Lorenzo rolled his eyes.

"Of course you'd say that."

After a pause Volker piped up and said, "There's another thing. I talked to my parents about studying music and I took your advice."

"What did they say?" Lorenzo tilted his head.

"They still don't like the idea of me studying music at a university, but they were more okay with it when I suggested I could also study business or instrument repair after I graduate as a fallback plan," the badger said and looked up at the stars. "At least now they're okay with me going into a music performance program."

"I know you don't want to teach so those sound like good ideas," Lorenzo said earnestly.

"Maybe after I get my degree I'll just do auditions or even go for a master's." Volker smirked.

"If things don't work out I'll be there for you, and if things get really bad we can live with my dad," Lorenzo said and laced his fingers with Volker's.

"That's good to know. We've got another year of Gymnasium and then the Abitur test. After that we'll be somewhere." Volker gently squeezed Lorenzo's paw.

"I'll go wherever you go. A lot of universities have math programs."

"Really? You don't want to study in Italy?"

"Well, I've never written a real essay in Italian. They've all been in German, besides the ones I've written for English and French class. Plus, I know mathematical terms better in German too. I'm so angry at myself for forgetting so much Italian."

"Don't you talk to your dad in Italian?"

"I do, but that's not the same as academic language, and I want to be with you. I guess the vocabulary we use when we're twelve isn't the same as when we go to a university. It's so frustrating. I have to go to a university in a country where people will be rude to me, work there, and live there for the rest of my life. I call myself Italian because I was born there, but now my world consists of German culture. I have no idea what's even going on in Italy these days; I have no real connections there. I don't even know what I'm supposed to be," Lorenzo said, massaging his temples.

"To me, you're the sweetest otter in the whole world, and I think you belong here," Volker said and placed their interwoven paws to his chest.

The two took a few minutes to enjoy the calm air as one boy stargazed and the other watched the water ripples around his feet.

A new piece started up from the town square. The beat was slower and the bassline was heavier. A cry of a single trumpet soared through the air and soon the rest of the brass instruments followed. The warm legato notes and wavy slurs created a romantic, cozy mood in the air.

"Would you care to dance?" Volker asked Lorenzo as he put his black paw out.

"Just don't step on my feet okay?" the otter smirked as their paws reunited.

"I'm not *that* clumsy," the badger replied as he helped Lorenzo up.

Lorenzo sank into his boyfriend's chest as the two of them danced slowly rocking against one another. The otter's soaked feet made wet paw prints that shone against the light of the streetlamps. They let the warm jazz overcome their senses and surround them. Swaying under the glow of the moon and the glimmer of the stars, they felt themselves harmonize with the world around them.

THE FORGIVENESS HEX

George Squares

ACAPULCO, MEXICO

Lupe was up early that morning, but who could blame her? She had been waiting weeks for this day and practiced her songs three times a day, every day since January. It had to mean something that the colors of the sky over Acapulco were red, orange, and yellow that morning—those were the colors of her plumage. She didn't want to presume it was a preemptive congratulation from an angel, or even Jesus, because pride like that was a sin. She had only hoped that it might be God's way of noticing her hard work, like a subtle, indirect message only she could decipher if she paid close attention. Lupe believed that God only spoke to those who listened or knew how to listen. He was charming in that way: mysterious and romantic. He rewarded the patient and the thoughtful, and he punished the people who demanded his messages in blunt, base clarity.

People like Eduardo Rodriguez. From the bus stop atop of the dunes, he stared at her now, giving her an ungodly crow. He was a cock in the literal and figurative sense. Deciding this thought was a sin, the lovebird whispered silent prayers to herself, standing on one leg as she rotated the rosary bound tightly to her leg.

"If I had that cousin of yours, I would be praying too!" he mocked. "It's lucky for you that you're named after the virgin mother."

Lupe cocked her head and then hopped up the dune. The silky sun-touched sand was just barely warm under her feet. Lupe passed Eduardo, hopping through the brush to reach the street and the bus stop. The sidewalk was pleasantly toasty when her talons descended.

She shifted her weight, letting her bag with her books slip off-kilter to the side of her back. Considering how practiced she was at this dance with Eduardo, she wondered why it wasn't the routine she had picked for the talent show. She adjusted her distance as Eduardo strutted towards her just slightly, enough to be annoying but not close enough for her to step on his talons.

The rooster cleared his throat. "I saw her in the graveyard this Saturday. She had a cup of *mate dulce,* you know, like she was going to offer the skeletons a sip after digging them up or something. Aren't your parents embarrassed?"

"I don't see why we have to speak about *my* family, when *your* father, he drinks and gambles his money away, and he shamelessly flirts with wives in front of their husbands. He will be in prison or worse before long if he doesn't change his ways."

Eduardo clicked his tongue. "But you see, my family, we are drinkers. We always have been. I probably will be too. As for prison, it would not be my father's first time. I think he would do well there. Your family drinks too, but they have a lot of money, and they do it in their *hacienda,* so it's okay. They also cheat on their wives, probably with each other, when they are not pedaling coke."

Lupe bobbed her head and let out a mirthful whistle. "Aha! So it is coke this time."

"But what they don't do," said the rooster, ignoring that

she had said anything at all, "is make conversation with the dead. My father's friends, they say to him, 'What has a great family like the Naranjos done to have a daughter stricken with madness?'"

Lupe's feathers ruffled. "Eliana is not mad—she's just strange. The poor girl, she lives in her fantasies and loses herself in her art. She has very few friends so she has to make ones up."

"Oh really?" Eduardo let out a scratchy laugh. "My father's friends, you should hear how they talk about the Naranjos now! Have they fallen from grace? Is this *bruja* the true punishment for their thievery and their swindling? Do they rub wings with the devil himself?"

A noisy puttering of gas interrupted their argument as a dirty, beat up steel bus rolled to a stop in front of them. A loud piston blew, and the door opened.

"Your bus has arrived," said Lupe, nonchalantly.

"I am surprised you know what a bus is, considering your family has servants to drive their cars for them. But perhaps they are teaching you things at that Catholic school after all. Later, *chica*."

When he was gone, she had to stand on one leg again. The sins she had thought up were more violent this time, so she made sure to pray double. This wasn't the first time somebody had approached her about Eliana. "*Bruja, bruja, bruja!*" they'd chant at her in whispers, but her cousin never seemed to care. She was aloof and serene, bedecked in her colorful shawls and her wild, huge straw hat, which had fresh flowers picked and woven into it nearly every day. Lupe decided that perhaps it was best to have a talk with her cousin about this when she got to school.

***

At lunch time, Lupe found Eliana in the art room like always. Her cousin didn't share her bright colors—Eliana's face plumage was white where Lupe's was a radiant orange, and her neck was like gray ash while Lupe's was sunshine yellow. The only hint of color Eliana's plumage had was her wing tips, which were pale gold.

"Good afternoon, cousin," said Lupe.

"Be careful. I am working with glaze. This kind will stain clothes. Trust me on that. I've lost more than one throw to this messiness." Eliana wore the standard girl's white vest for St. Aloysius that they all had to wear, but she still had that wild straw sun hat upon her head, even indoors. She donned a *mantilla* over her shoulders, which was milky white with a lacy hem made up of finely knitted gardenias.

Lupe clicked her tongue at her cousin's wardrobe. "Then perhaps you shouldn't wear such fancy things when you're working on art. Or, I suppose, just because you want to flaunt against the authority of the dress code."

"Oh this?" Eliana gave a cursory glance at her shoulder. "Nobody has given me trouble for this. Only compliments."

"Or words you only take to be compliments, cousin. You say that nobody has given you trouble, but that is not true. Your troubles have come to me. People talk about you."

Spinning the pottery wheel with one talon on the pedal, Eliana carved out a spiral with a chisel she held in place with her other foot. She left leaf indentations and carnations in the urn. "It is a school. Everyone talks about one another. And I only hear the loveliest things about you. I think these words are much more valuable than the words of bored people who only want to add excitement into their lives when they have none."

Lupe whistled excitedly. "So, what you are saying is, it is a brazen lie when people say you drift into graveyards and they hear you try to speak to the departed?"

The spinning wheel stopped. "I only speak to them because I have heard them speak. They never make sense, so I don't think they can hear me, but I know they are trying to say something. They're so incredibly sad. So sad that I know I want to help them... You know, if you tried, you could probably hear them better. But you haven't tried, so it is up to me."

Lupe flapped her wings irritably and hopped. "This is exactly what I mean. You speak nonsense as if it were mundane truth, and then you expect people to treat you kindly. When you lie like that to a person's face, they think you consider them stupid. It is insulting!"

The pottery wheel started turning again. "*Perdón.* I did not mean to make you angry, cousin. But you'd know how I felt if you heard them. It is like they are stuck. Sometimes in their own misery, sometimes in a dance they enjoyed. I don't know if I can make them unstuck."

"Your mother would be ashamed if she heard you talking about that. You know that all spirits are in heaven or hell."

"But there is Limbo. I think it might be something like this. Like where those poor voices are."

"It is dangerous—more importantly, sacrilegious, to think we know more about Limbo than a priest."

"Which is why I have spoken to Father Munez about it. And Sister Luciana."

Those words were like an anchor at Lupe's feet. She had told the schoolmasters about this? Her lungs inflated with air as she tried to calm herself with one deep breath. If they knew, then everybody must truly know by now. They might start calling Eliana a graverobber. Or worse, they could call her a necrophiliac. *Bruja, bruja, bruja* echoed in her head. She looked about the art room, and everything about it made her angry. Eliana's shelf was covered in rows and rows of cellophane flowers or terracotta sugar skulls. Her cousin had once even made a statuette of Quetzalcoatl, but they wouldn't let her put it in the kiln. Lupe was sure that everybody remembered this, too. It felt like Eliana was a child who couldn't leave her nest, consumed with the stories their grandmother used to tell, probably hearing the voices of demons through the friendly disguise of childhood fondness she couldn't let go of. It made Lupe sad and afraid, but mostly frustrated.

"Why don't you come with me to the computer lab?" said Lupe, suddenly noticing the high tone in her own voice. "We can set you up on Facebook. That way it will be easier to talk to people your age. I know you've never been to a concert, and I just wouldn't want you to miss out on a lot of great things."

Eliana tittered. "I don't worry about those silly things. I have tried the Facebook before. It is mostly people complaining about why they can't do things. I would rather do things. Even if you say they aren't popular."

"I just don't want to see you left behind!" Lupe shrieked. "We are supposed to be growing up and you are not!" Her voice echoed off of the walls. She blushed and looked out behind her. Some students started walking again when they saw her gaze. Now she was trembling with humiliation.

The ashen bird sighed. "Okay, I will open up the Facebook again, and I will try to be sociable there. I promise. *Perdón.*"

"*Gracias,*" was all Lupe could manage to say before hopping out of the art room. The great iron church bell was ringing, signaling the end of the lunch period, when something soft touched her shoulder.

Sister Luciana loomed over her. The doe had a graceful air about her and gave the lovebird a beatific smile. Her black habit was always immaculate, and she wore long white gloves that covered her hoof-like hands. "I'm glad I caught you before your English class. I need to speak with you in my office."

Lupe experienced a sinking feeling. "Yes, *señora.*"

Sister Luciana's office was lofty, sparse and filled with stained glass windows. There were mahogany tables holding a few lamps that looked like candlesticks and a bowl full of tamarind candy precariously placed near an edge. The only piece of technology was a small computer sitting on Luciana's desk, turned at a corner, so that Lupe could barely see that the screen was filled with spreadsheets.

Luciana made little noise when she took her seat at her desk. "I hope you've had a pleasant day so far, *bambina,*" she said kindly. "I rarely have to see you, considering you're an excellent student, but I'm sure you know that already."

Lupe *did* know this. She always tried so hard to study, to

do her work, and to practice her singing that she feared it came off as natural talent. It was constant effort, always, to be the best that God might intend her to be. She nodded at the nun. The nun smiled warmly. "So, drop your guard. This is not a disciplinary meeting. There is nothing to be alarmed about here. Would you like some candy?"

Lupe did want some candy, but not today. "I might cut my tongue on something sharp if I'm not careful. Especially tonight."

"The pageant, of course." The doe's eyes shone with understanding. "I took second place in my year when I played the organ. I had never been so happy to win second place. The stress was terrible. When I was a girl, I knew when the audience looks at us and sees a sequined gown, they see bubbly young women, but when we look at ourselves, we see skyscrapers made out of steel, scouring for cracks in the infrastructure." She smiled again. "And then when it's over, we all let ourselves fall like the Tower of Babel. It's the most relieving feeling: casting off that hubris. But things turned back to normal when it was over."

"I hope I do not come across as arrogant." Lupe hesitated. "I thought this was not a disciplinary meeting."

"It is not. But you do point out I'm rambling. This is about your cousin."

Lupe looked back and forth. "I think she is a good person, and she's trying her best."

"But you're worried that her best isn't enough and that it will make you look bad?"

Lupe's tail feathers rustled. "It is not a worry so much as a reality. She's obsessed with macabre things! She collects bones and replicates them in drawings and clay. She's been seen near people's dead loved ones in the middle of the night. I fear things like this are why she can't make friends so easily."

The doe nodded. "Strange, sure, but most girls are strange in their teens. And I've seen stranger. I *will* see stranger. But she is also remarkably kind and thoughtful. She always has the most observant things to say in her literature courses. I'd say she's gifted and… strong. Wouldn't you agree?"

"Gifted?" This was legitimately confusing to hear. "She makes up fantasies to make herself seem more interesting. Shouldn't we be trying to help her break these habits rather than encouraging them? How will she ever learn to change if she thinks she can wear whatever accessories she likes when nobody else can?"

The doe flinched, as if caught off guard, but then steadied her composure. "We've already talked to your aunt and uncle and the other instructors. The circumstances are… unusual, but she is allowed to wear her hat and her shawl."

"You do realize why she wears that hat, don't you? And why she adorns it with fresh flowers every day?"

The doe sighed. "Do you believe what the other girls say then? *Bruja?*"

"No, I am too old to believe in witches," said Lupe carefully, "but I know pagan rituals when I see them. It just makes me very sad to see sacrilegious behaviors praised, even encouraged, in a Catholic institution."

Sister Luciana held up a gloved hand. "But you also have to realize that Christianity wasn't the first religion in this country. I believe that you don't win the minds and hearts of people by telling them they cannot do things. You show them that you live better. That you are happy with yourself. I think Eliana is very happy with herself."

Lupe shook her head. "I'm sorry, but I cannot find that to be an acceptable answer. You tell me that being happy with yourself is most important, but we are entrenched in a world of rules. If we sin, we must atone. We must follow a dress code. We must attend church on the Sabbath, and we must accept Christ as our savior or else face hellfire. If you, a nun who has taken unto herself the biggest rule that a woman can take, to marry God and not man, and to never lay with one, tells me that rules are not so consequential—then who can say my priorities are misguided? Perhaps I am not the one who is confused, sister."

Sister Luciana looked shocked. "Enough." Luciana's voice could cut steel. Her eyes slit and she looked over the girl. "I see your reasoning, and do not deny its virtue, but to think you could be so cold at time like this is most inappropriate."

Lupe tilted her head. "At a time like what?"

The doe pulled back, as if she had begun to realize something she previously hadn't.

"I think it is not my place to intervene any longer. Eliana's condition is a school affair, although apparently not a family one." Luciana rose from her desk. "You are dismissed. I wish you luck at the pageant tonight."

***

When Lupe went home after school, she was confused by what Sister Luciana had said. She wanted to ask her mother about it, but her office was locked, and Lupe could hear that she was busy with bookkeeping duties.

But Lupe also hadn't practiced singing all day. The pageant was that night, and she couldn't let something so cryptic distract her. Perhaps tomorrow, but certainly not tonight. She had to ground herself in her music.

She puffed up, air filled her lungs, and then she tweeted, stringing together chains of notes while she applied red eye shadow to her face and cheek glitter that smelled like fresh citrus.

She spent hours getting ready. Staring into the mirror, she still felt imperfect, but her time had run out and her mother was calling for her. She left with her parents in their limousine, staring at the bay for any sort of hint God might leave her about winning the pageant. She stared at the reflection of the light in the bay and thought how, perhaps, she could use that.

***

Lupe was sure there were several thousand heads in the auditorium that night. Parents, children and business owners filled the rows.

When it was Lupe's time to perform, they called her number. She made sure not to stare into the spotlights when she moved past the periwinkle blue curtains and onto the stage. All eyes were on her, but she treated every glassy gaze just like the flickering flames from her bathroom candles.

She raised her wings to heaven and sang her first note. Something high, then something low, to show off her vocal range: trills and warbles that rang like clarion bells, precise in their choice of note, never faltering. She sang the way a general would lay out his tactics, treating every decision as life or death, to show them all she would never know shame.

She moved with her music too. Like bright light passing through water, she sparkled, and her gait flowed with her rhythm of her tune, beckoning all she could reach into the harmony of her sound.

And then it was over, months of practice culminating in two minutes' time. The audience roared with applause. She bowed to the judges, not wanting to overstay her welcome. Head high and wings low, she hopped away, happy for the first time in months, knowing she had given her best. She found her mother in the audience, crying tears of joy, and embraced her. Nothing could ruin this moment.

Nothing until Eliana stepped onto the stage. The blue spotlights made her plumage glow, and she walked as a dead beast might, stiff, and slow as her shawl shifted with the weight of her shoulders.

"Hello. My name is Eliana, and I don't usually do pageants." She trudged toward the microphone and tilted it downward so that it reached her beak. "I don't know if I can get through all that I want to say, but I'm going to try. It's a personal monologue." Lupe stared at the stage from the audience. Being a fool at school was one thing but she picked tonight, of all nights, to act like her bizarre self. Lupe didn't know if she'd ever forgive Eliana for this.

"I want to talk today a little about… theology. In a respectful way. As it seems, I've picked up something of a reputation for myself without even trying to. I've built elaborate *ofrendas* for my deceased relatives, because I believe in honoring the dead, as my family has before me, for centuries.

"And not just on *Dia de los Muertos*." She lifted a foot, staggered, and then stomped to balance herself. "Some people say that I speak to the dead. Talk at is probably closer to the truth, considering there isn't exactly very much open communication when you're attempting a dialogue with a skeleton." The audience laughed at her. Lupe didn't think they were laughing *with* her. They couldn't be.

"Most all of us, if not all of us, are Catholic here tonight. I know that our religion mentions spirits. The Holy Spirit, at the very least, although I do not know what it means to connect with such a force. Existing as he does according to our religion, his voice does not speak directly with you. In the same way, a ghost has never spoken directly with me." Eliana looked at both sides of the audience now, her expression utterly solemn.

"Many girls in my year have called me *bruja*, although I do not think they mean it, nor do I really understand what such a term means." The audience was utterly quiet now.

"Usually, in many of the stories I read, when a girl is wrongfully accused of being a witch, it means she is special. The town takes their fear into their own hands. Often they kill her. Then the girl returns as a demon or a spirit and enacts grisly retribution upon those who has wronged her. But I am not special, and I am not a witch." He eyes were half lidded, and she was rocking back and forth.

"I have nothing against any of you. I just have a simple message, before I am finished: that ghosts as we understand them do not exist."

Eliana wrapped both of her wings around the microphone stick, sliding down until she crumpled to the floor, looking like a pile of snow dusted with crimson. There were a few awkward golf claps from the audience, and the judges looked confused. The curtains never closed. Suddenly there were a few rumbles of concern from the crowd and then a cry. It came from her own mother. "Why are you all standing there? Go help her! Something's wrong!" Lupe just stared at her cousin's body, seeing no signs of breath. A few parents scrambled to the stage.

"She doesn't have a heartbeat."

"What do you mean she doesn't have a heartbeat? She was talking just minutes ago!"

As Lupe stared and stared, her vision of Eliana was blocked when more parents piled onto the stage. Sirens wailed in the distance while she heard the most horrible sound she had heard in her life. A voice that was but also wasn't Eliana's echoed from the stage where her body lie. It was distorted, as if produced by a broken radio. Nobody else could seem to hear it, and it echoed inside of Lupe's head. *Perdón, cousin. This might be the only way to make it work, if it did work.*

Lupe ran from the auditorium. She ran until she could flap her wings, riding a thermal into the sky, purple and black and mottled with stars without even the faintest trace of any sun. She could not bear to be at that place any longer. She just needed to fly and then fall asleep in her own bed, under her covers until the sun was up again.

***

A week after Eliana's death, on a day where the sky was colored halcyon, and the clouds puffed up like cotton, Lupe attended the funeral at the Naranjos' family tomb. Not because she was forced to, but because she wanted to make sure she had heard Eliana's ghost that night.

She wore a black shawl and hat that matched her mother's. Eliana's side of the family was dressed in bright reds, blues and yellows, bedecked in carnations and roses on stringed necklaces. Lupe counted about fifty bright colored heads hopping together, spreading their wings as they turned while other family members played the guitar, the maracas and the tambourine. Sister Luciana was there too, wearing her plain black habit and holding a bouquet of carnations in her hand, speaking to Aunt Verónica and Eliana's mother.

"Thank you for doing as much for her as you could," said the squat bird with the stony face who always smelled like burnt sugar. "We knew the spinal cancer would take her and it had been years."

Luciana nodded and dabbed at her eyes with a kerchief. "I did not understand her wishes at first. I nearly ruined them."

"She wouldn't have wanted anybody to treat her differently," said Aunt Verónica. "It was her time, and I don't think she would have had this any other way."

"We had spent so much money on procedures and still nothing," said Lupe's mother, fiddling with her pearls. "I just wish there was more we could have done."

Aunt Verónica shook her head. "She wouldn't have let you. She told me she didn't want to be in a hospital when it happened. She faced death just as bravely as mother did. I was blessed to have her as long as I did. Longer than those asshole doctors projected."

Lupe's mother embraced Aunt Verónica. "Eliana and mother were strong in that way. Stronger than me, anyway. I am proud of our daughters. I always will be."

"I'll always be proud of our babies. Even the ones who aren't here anymore." Aunt Verónica sniffed.

Luciana caught Lupe's gaze and gave her a kind smile. "Congratulations on first place in the pageant, *bambina*. Or should I say, *señorita*? I haven't had the opportunity to congratulate you since…" She nodded at the funeral party.

Lupe could not find words, so she only bowed and hopped away from the music and the crowds of adults. She certainly did not feel like a winner, even though she gave her best and won. How could she feel good after any outcome, after that night? How could the adults not tell her that Eliana was sick for that long? Luciana tried, but… it had been against Eliana's wishes, as well as the rest of the family who knew. Everyone's except her own, of course. They thought she had lacked the strength to know.

After the service was over, Lupe visited her family's tomb. It was pleasantly dry with rays of sunlight penetrating the opening of the mausoleum roof. Red, white and yellow carnations scattered the top of Eliana's sarcophagus, and the lit wicks of candles flickered from Lupe's movements.

"Okay Eliana, I'm here to listen," said Lupe. Her voice echoed slightly in the chamber. After waiting for minutes, she found no response.

"You spoke to me before at the pageant. I know you're there." She waited an hour this time. Dust motes floated past beams of light. She stared at the flowers long enough to wilt before she picked up her bag and hopped out into the sunlight. Lupe never heard her cousin's voice again, but she always listened. Listened. Listened for the voice she knew she heard.

Vanillupus and Other People's Wits Take on the Inhospitable World

Slip Wolf

Prince Patrick Island, Canada

I met them both in Paris, but forgot their names in Tokyo. Details, details. The leopardess is an entertainment news anchor, six years in the business and around the world a few times. She interviewed me between shows, and I debriefed her between sheets. She holds her liquor well. Her camera guy, a solid-stacked horse, handles himself as well as he handles his eight-foot boom mike. He came with us after the interview wrapped up. What can I say? The music industry is very tight knit at all pay grades. Too bad that while I'm sure her name is Mandy Styles or Wiles, I can't remember his at all. The empty cognac bottle rolling back and forth across my plane's bedroom compartment probably has something to do with that.

None of us were belted in last night. I'm sure it was slumber-time turbulence that has two of us and three sheets—also to the wind as they say—now crammed up against the starboard bulkhead. My blue-dyed bushy tail is kinked, landed on it at least once. The runic symbols up and down my torso fur are matted and mussed. My tongue runs across my dry nose. I sense that we've landed in SFO. Awesome. We can get to the hotel in time to shower and maybe have a little more fun before randy Mandy and her handy assistant grab a rental back down the coast to LA.

Somebody groans. I see a bit of horse flank and am impressed with how artfully the last twisted sheet has given modesty back to video-horse. Wiles—or was it Delisles—straight up, I can't be sure about her first name either—is curled up next to me against the curving bulkhead. She's awake, looking relieved.

My head throbs a bit in her golden-eyed gaze and I smile. "Nevada's just a hop and a skip from here. Want to be stupid and get married?" I flash canines and realize she's not smiling back. Which ex's name did I scream out this time?

"We tried to wake you. I had Nausica slap you around a bit, but you didn't budge through either landing. I didn't know a husky could sleep so soundly."

"Either landing?" I blink as I try to count the number of landings a single stop flight should have. Then do it again to make sure. Head really hurts. "Did we run out of fuel or something?"

"We hit a storm six hours out of Paris, remember? You had us jumping up and down on the bed when the turbulence came. The co-pilot lost his shit."

I didn't remember that. Wait, I remembered that intern marten in flight-blues screaming at me. That happened. Then Mandy bouncing, so much bouncing.

She snapped her fingers next to my ear. "Pay attention. We had to make an emergency landing in Anchorage."

"That in Vancouver?" Christ, I needed a coffee. With Irish whiskey and whipped cream. That would help get my shit together.

The leopardess's spots crinkled as she frowned at me, such a cute frown. "That's Alaska, rockstar."

"That was my next guess."

The horse, Nausica, I now recall, moaned and rolled over, one hoof kicking.

"So we went on our way—"

"And ran into another storm along the coast, which redirected us, again—"

"Man, sounds like a hell of a story. At least we touched down."

"—further north. The storm was something like six hundred miles long and deep into Canada."

My head's full on pounding now. I shakily get to my feet, letting the bedsheet fall to the ground. My blond fur is cold in the cabin's over-cranked air as I turn to the window. "So when did we finally get to San Fran—" Through the frosty window I can see white and more white. Broken here and there by the blue of bare, wicked ice. Glaciers.

"We didn't, Van." The leopard sighs. Under the blanket, she's mostly clothed again. "We're in the southern lip of the Arctic circle, Prince Patrick Island to be exact."

There's silence, save a snort from Nausica. He rolls on his back, revealing the beer bottle labels he'd stuck to his muscular chest as he knocked them back like some sort of tattoo collage. Seven lagers, two dark ales. Impressive. I turn back to the frost-lined window "We're where?" My throat's so dry I squeak.

"Dammit, Jack up in the cockpit said you'd be like this. How do you even get it together to do shows?"

"I don't. That's why they're awesome." I stumble to the night table and open the latched drawer to fish for Tylenol. "I've got a media scrum at two, then practice at three. What time is it?"

"Forget it. We're a nine-hour flight from San Fran at this point, and the satellite phone won't work. This is a disused landing strip set up by some Canadian research expedition that watched penguin fisherman play lacrosse or something." She frowns. "Something seems odd about that. Anyway, they have enough fuel to get us down to Edmonton which has its airport buried under that raging storm. We're stranded here, probably for days."

It hits me. "No. No! Vanillupus doesn't miss a show. Illnesses, rashes, custody hearings, all irrelevant. It's not just a slogan, it's the way the universe flows."

Mandy growls in a way that's almost canine. "It's geography. We had to reroute twice, and I spent three straight hours through the worst of the storm fearing for my life in Nausica's arms."

That hurt. "Why not my arms?"

"You were passed out during the worst of it, moron!"

It hurts even to shrug. Not just emotionally. "Well..."

Nausica snorts again and there's a knock at the hatch.

"Come in," I mutter.

"Is everybody decent?" Jack's muffled voice asks from the forward cabin

"Does it matter?"

My weasel pilot for the last few years enters. I hired Jack in the Sky Lounge at Frankfurt after he found out his former airline folded with an hour's notice. That and a couple drinks turned his frown upside-down. "Do we need the kit?"

"No bandages, nor smelling salts." I look at the heavily slumbering, sticker-chested horse. "For us anyway. Status report, Captain?" I turn, forgetting I'm naked, but remembering Jack's used to that.

"We bought as much fuel as they'd sell us, barely enough to get to the next airport south of here. With the storm still on, I can't risk it. Nathan's also worried about getting us properly de-iced to fly."

"Fuck. So how long are we stranded?"

Jack sighs. "Spring up here starts in three months, maybe. At least I was able to radio out and let everybody know you're alive. Your agent says Twitter is blowing up right now."

"Such dedicated fans." I sigh.

"Actually, they're all pissed off that your show may be canceled." Jack shrugs.

"Same thing."

"So how the hell are we getting out of here?" Mandy asks.

"I can maybe help you wit dat," chips a voice over Jack's shoulder. A penguin stuffs himself past the weasel, flap-capped and plaid wool wrapped. "Hey, I live on da floe over der wit da chimney and da hockey sticks. Family's been 'ere, oh, seventy years I'd specken."

"Cool." I don't know what else to say. "I'm Vanillupus, the EDM artist."

The penguin cocks his head. "Artist, eh? Sounds really great mister blue-dye doggo. Who de spotty kitty?"

"This is Mandy—"

"I'm Julia Braun with Spinlist News."

I try not to frown. "I thought your name was Mandy."

Her eyes narrow. "I know. You shouted it out twice last night. Mandy is my counterpart at Coastal Colossus." She grins at the penguin while giving me the stink-eye. The squat bird reaches out a flipper and daintily pecks a kiss on her proffered paw. "And you are?" she asks.

"Linny. Short for Linnikoo. Its penguin for shiny ice, don'tcha know?"

"I didn't."

"Do now!" He squawks a laugh that makes my head throb even more. Julia and Jack laugh with him. Nausica snorts.

Julia's smile gives way to a frown again. "Something's a little...weird. You're a penguin, right?"

"Right-e-oh."

"I'm not positive about this, but aren't penguins native to the Antarctic? This is the completely opposite hemisphere."

I struggle to focus. I don't remember any arctic with ants in it, but alcohol is still blanking out the parts that don't help me breathe. "Yeah?"

Linny glances from her to me and back. "Oh, right. Well, we did da migration."

Julia's eyes widen. "You migrated up here?"

"Yeah, we wanted to live near some friends of ours, a tribe of toucans over the next ice floe der."

"Umm—"

"Soo I unnerstand yous all have a mackeral in da brine here. A real snafoo with da music show you wanna get to and stoof like that. Ya need to get sooth."

Julia's brow creased. "Oh, South! To Edmonton, yes. Then further."

"Well, sounds like a doozy wit da storm ragin' hard. How's bout you come down to the shack where da other guests are and we can make all yoos some grub for brekky."

Julia and Jack both sigh with relief as Nausica stirs awake, one eye opening wanly. I shrug and put a comradely paw on the penguin's shoulder. "I'm starved, myself. Got any eggs?"

***

It's colder than a fish's tit in a sardine ice cream tub outside. I'm wearing three layers of athletic gear, a leather jacket and a borrowed knit hat. Julia and Jack shiver with me. Nausica, now awake, looks irritated if anything. A squad of penguins slide around on the ice throwing a ball with what looked like snowshoes on poles. I don't know winter games, but I think it's curling or hockey, maybe. Had I held back to get more details my eyes would have frozen. That would have been the second time that ever happened and the first without over-proof vodka. Sweden makes the coldest places warm, let me tell you.

Here it's just miserable. Every breath out of my mouth is a ghost that freezes to death and hits the snowy path until we get inside. It takes ten full minutes for my limbs to return to life and even then, it's pins and needles from tail to snout. Winter sucks is what I'm getting at. Don't care if I'm a Husky, that's just a stereotype.

I try to keep Julia as warm as she is already getting in Nausica's broad arms. I'm not jealous. If anything, I want to join them. This time preferably around a roaring fire.

In here, a couple space heaters have to do. We're not alone. Two young penguins toss sardines from a bowl in the air and swallow them whole on the way down at one table. At another sits a white ursine colossus whose head is brushing the low metal ceiling. I'm talking a foot on Nausica big. The polar bear blows on some steaming soup that looks pretty good.

Behind a kitchen window, a penguin in a white smock waves a flipper and points at a cursory meal list with prices. They'd better take plastic. Julia is already ordering a salmon burger or something.

I wander over to the polar bear as something sizzles on the skillet. "Hey friend?" Large dark eyes drift silently up to mine. "Nice little village you got here."

"They."

"Huh?"

"They got here. I'm not a local. Just passing through, actually. Well I was before I got stranded."

Right away that doesn't sound good. "Oh. You a fisherman? Or a shack builder? Or whatever else they have up here?"

The bear's paw stops halfway to a gaping mouth and pained eyes look balefully back. "I'm Addison Bruinster Sinclair, a professional explorer and extreme sports junkie. Have a couple Guinness World Records for base jumping and one for powerboating. Remember that windsail over an active Hawaiian lava stream last year that needed a skyhook extraction before it touched down on four thousand degree lava? The cam footage got sixty million views on YouTube. I was also an honorary mention at the Darwin Awards, so I decided to take it easy this year. Just your average sub-zero Northern passage run with a boat, sail, outboard solid rocket booster for the fun part, and some protein shakes." The bear shrugged expansively. "It was a calm, steady progress. Ocean smooth as glass when my malfunctioning radar told me I had a clear a two hundred-mile lane to hit my desired sixty knots per hour. So I figured, 'Awesome, let's do this!' Should have seen before I lit the candle that the low cloud far ahead was in fact a displaced glacier. Anyway, I dived overboard in time, but with the hull sunk. I'm stranded until the next supply mission from Nunavut."

"Wow. That just sucks. Still you must feel right at home here, really in your element, huh."

The bear frowns. "No. I'm from Santa Rosa."

"A polar bear from Santa Rosa? Like, California?"

"People can be from other places. It's the twenty-first century; we have boats and planes and real estate listings. Didn't you see the penguins? And why would I want to be here, ancestral home or not? I've been soaked in freezing water, buried in snow for weeks and was scared out of my freaking mind for most of it. Also, I'm—"

"Wow, my man. Again, sucks."

"Thanks." The bear looks annoyed. What is it with people and the side-eye today? The bear takes a slow slurp of soup. "At least when the pontoons kept floating, the cargo nets kept some of the gear that wasn't pulverized from sinking. I've got no boat now, but the satellite uplink on my helmet camera array stayed with me and is working fine. My emergency beacon went off and the Canadian Navy was on its way, but I went on-stream in camp here and told them I was fine and safe for now. So they turned around and told me they'd be up next month. Shouldn't have told them my careening rocket took out the Tim Hortons shack, which is how this camp knew to look for me in the first place. Vindictive bastards, those Canadians. Who knew."

I clap the pour soul on the back. "Strapping guys like yourself and I have more ability to overcome adversity in situations like this. Unlike the fairer sexes, like Julia over there."

"Um…" Addision says flatly.

"I learned a while ago that when the champagne is getting

warm and flat in the penthouse party the label is holding and they ask you if you want another, you don't say 'It's okay, I'll finish this one.' Yeah, honesty can hurt you. I feel your pain."

"Really, you're gonna compare—"

"Whatever. Life's a bitch and we endure. I'm Vanillupus. You probably know my work."

The bear blinks up at me. "Yeah, I guessed with the blue fur dye and runes and stuff. And, well, the attitude. They play your music at the X-games all the time. To be honest I'm much more partial to A-fox Twin, no offense. Although some of the sharp bass drops in your songs are really, uh, loud, like just seismically penetrating."

"No offense taken, and thanks for the oddly specific compliment. So, uh, the Navy is coming up to get you, right?"

"At some point. They don't have an ice-breaker they can reroute that can cut through that passage-blocking slippage right now. It's like ten feet tall, although my rocket boat did put a big crack in it. I'm actually getting myself mentally focused while I wait, planning my next stunt, decorating an igloo the penguin's helped me make where I've stacked the pontoons that didn't sink and mediating on warm tropical places where it's not extremity-snap-off freezing. Or moderate forested ones. Really can't have picky fantasies up here."

A shiver on top of all the other shivers runs through me. "Yeah, totally not. Be right back."

A trudge over to my crew finds them already in worse spirits. "How the hell can it be this cold indoors?" Nausica rumbles, both Jack and Julia huddled up next to him for warmth. They stare into their hot cocoas glumly. "I found out the radio here is on the fritz. We've only the one on the plane to let them know what our status is."

"Still alive. I was able to get out that much. I'm just worried the plane won't stay de-iced long enough to take off when the storm's done," Jack adds bitterly.

"I'd like to get the hell out of here," I say, tail limp on the cold wooden floor. "Where's your intern, Jack?"

"Nathan is my co-pilot, not an intern, Van," Jack replies with a frown. "He finished with the plane and went to talk to the mayor of this town, if that's what this is. There's a couple other shacks like this near here that seem to be part of past Canadian expeditions. One of them has been turned into a makeshift hotel and bar according to Linny."

Speak of the tuxedoed devil, Lin waddles up. "Howdy do der. Ya'll get some stew or sumtin?"

Julia swallowed from her mug. "We're cold but feeling a bit better. We'd really love a place to get warm."

"Talk ta me brother. Eee's a wiz wit da blow-torch anna steel siding and used two old shacks to make one big super shack up da hill der. Got a heater and a wit bar. S'okay place if ye like board games and VCR box sets a' Littlest Hobo. Poor bro has all dis equipment and nothing left to build wit after dem CeeBeeCee people never came back with tourists. I was shocked when dat didn' happen. That Reck Mercer boyo looked like an honest feller."

"Do you have cognac?" I ask, horrified, looking for a silver lining anywhere I can.

"Don't know what cones ye mean. Yaks, yeah is speckon I saw what might be one a season back. Beeg fella, grunts alla time. Almost like yeer horsey friend 'ere."

Nausica sighs. "Can't we just stay back on the plane?"

"No," Jack says, affecting a thousand yard stare. "We need the limited electrical power to warm up the aircraft when we can fly. It's gonna get cold in there. But too cold and we won't be able to lift off without a boost. Takes a lot of power to do that, not just gas, and de-icing's no fun let me tell you."

"How's the storm doing," Julia asks hopefully.

"Hangin' on like a meanie house guest. Could come by again any time."

I pound the table in righteous anger. "I can't miss this gig. I can't miss! This! Gig! Adoring fans will be pissed. I'll be cold, and bored!"

"And what about the rest of us?" Julia growls, standing up

and thrusting a clawed finger in my direction. "What about the canned report we're supposed to submit about your new album? What about your pilot and co-pilot not freezing to death as they try to keep your precious plane halfway warm? All the money and fame and influence hasn't made you any less of a self-absorbed asshole. I almost regret sleeping with you!"

The shack goes dead silent, every smacking beak and slurping mouth close at once. Julia looks around, her tail curling under her, a blush comes to her ear tips.

"Remember, everybody." I point out. "She said almost."

I try to meet Nausica's eyes to see if he feels the same and the horse just looks down his extremely long face at me. "I loved hanging with you up until...this. Still, she's kinda right. You're a great recording artist, but you do little more than drink and bitch sometimes. It's cute, but also damn annoying to have to cut around in post."

I feel a weight on me as the words set in. I turn to Jack, my last port of sympathy in this storm.

The weasel is glum. "Look, I'm grateful that you financed my certification to keep flying. I'm also grateful for the first aid, CPR, craft distillery and pharmaceutical dispensary licensing courses you paid for me to take. But we never really talk. Hell, the only thing you even wanted to know about Nathan is whether his blood type is the same is yours."

Jack goes silent and all eyes are on me. I see their breath rise above the table in frozen puffs and realize I don't feel well. It's as though something is absent within myself that isn't drink and isn't adoration or the satisfaction that comes from a great studio session. A hollow space opens up inside, curling my whiskers and making my chest hurt.

A flipper touches my shoulder. "Hey, I could cheer you's up nice. Back win da T.V. sports people was watchin' dese here lacrosse games, dey left a sound system dat we keep for karaoke and council meets and udder things. It puts out a lot a power too, rattles de roof when it's full pop, near enough ta cause a landslide. Maybe ye want to play some o' dat music a yers, get yer mind offa how dreary ya find it. We just wanna be good hosts to yous all."

The flipper points at a tarped stack of something sitting forlornly against one wall. There's the grill of a massive Marshall speaker peaking from under the cover.

The bear lumbers up. "Couldn't help overhearing all that," Addison says. "You've gotta break this ice while you're ahead. I lost good friends due to my selfishness over the years, expecting everything to go my way because life was a bitch I had to fight with. I learned that you can't weld the people onto your life whom you cherish the most and float on from all those who don't serve your needs. Fame makes us into islands of solipsistic seclusion that we can never escape from. And not the fun tropical ones either."

The bear turns to regard the rest of the table. "Oh, Julia Braun with Spinlist! Hey, I watch your show all the time."

Julia manages a toothy, chattering smile. "Thank you so much. I loved your parasail base-jump off the cliffs of Dover in that Union Jack onesie you did for that Cubs Needing Cots charity marathon."

Addison smiles. "The kids loved it most of all. That was the important part."

"You're a hero to many."

"Oh stop," Addison says.

Yes stop, I think glumly, still caught in my self-pity and guilt in one deep snowy well that only threatens to become deeper as I fade into the background. Here I am, trapped thousands of miles from waiting fans in a polar purgatory with the skies unflyable, a giant ice floe blocking the only way out by boat and nobody loving me-let's not forget that part. Then there's the jumble of pontoons, film equipment, satellite gear, a welding apparatus, incredibly powerful speakers and amplifiers to taunt me.

Hang on a second.

"Linny."

"Yeah, doggo?"

"Your brother's a welder, right?"

"Jinny's darn good at it too. Studied away in de summer and brought his skills back 'ere. Kind of a folk 'ero."

"Would he like to be a hero again? Like a real one?"

***

"Wow, this could actually work." Julia's ears perk as she stands bundled under the bright but ineffectual sun at a days' worth of spot welding and rough labor. She keeps warm sandwiched between the large hulking frame of Addison and the large hard frame of Nausica to her right, camera mounted on his shoulder, filming. The breath of a dozen watchers rises slowly into the arctic sky as they stand around my tour plane. Or rather, what it has become.

"Not a bad bitta weldin' there, eh?" Speaks a familiar voice to my left.

I grin, tail wagging hard, a fifth of bourbon closing enough blood vessels that my ears don't feel that they're going to fall off. "Your brother Jinny did some sick welding there."

The penguin narrows his eyes at me. "I'm Jinny."

"Right. So, we good to go?"

"Electrics tested oot. The stuff is heavy duty, I can say. CeeBeeCee guys said they'd be back soom day far it all. Feckin' liars'll never show now dat da Timmies be blowed up."

"We'll bring it to them. And now that it's part of the greatest club experiment in the world, it'll belong in an art exhibit. Hell, this whole place will belong under glass after today!"

Jinny nods slowly, studying something far off. "Can't wait," he mutters.

Giddy for the first time in days, I call out to the plane's open hatch. "Ready?"

Jack leans out and holds his thumb up. "Come on board!"

One at a time, we head up the folding stairs, Julia, Nausica, Jinny, Linny and Addison. A larger group of penguins in assorted winter gear honks and trills from a nearby hillock of ice as the brothers wave goodbye. We crank the staircase up and close the hatch. I check out port and starboard wings where the speakers are strapped and welded down, feeding lines back into the cabin to the mixing and turntable station assembled in the main cabin in front of the bar. I pad confidently over behind the decks, mixers and laptop, checking the fittings. "Ready to start the show?"

"What song are you going to play out there?" Coat removed, Julia is in her host's desk best, black strapless ensemble looking both alluring and severe at once. Nausica is already recording, camera feed travelling a short line to the satellite uplink that Addison is running.

"We're kicking this set off with a remix of Metha-bone clinic! This shit is going to—what?"

Julia frowns. "Um, you've noticed that most of the village is on the hill. Some of the penguins are kinda small, Van."

"Cause they're far away right?"

Julia folds her arms and her black-lined ears flatten. "Because they're underaged penguin chicks, Van."

"Oh," I look at Linny and Vinny, who stand there innocuously. "'Kay then. Guess I should pull Double-parked Mange-Rover off the set list then."

"Just maybe you should," Julia grumbles.

"Let's play Bermuda try-an-angle then. No lyrics, just a deep lush forest of psychedelic ambience with crisply layered drum kits stretching to percussive infinity. Or that's what the Knotdrop review called it. So nice of them. Author was a cutie."

"As long as it has the right bass hit when we need it," Addison pipes up.

"Oh, don't you worry. Hey Jack, we're cleared for takeoff!"

"On it," comes the call back from the cockpit. The engines sputter to life, having been de-iced one last time. As they warm up to full power, the plane begins to slide forward. It can't roll, as the wheels have been removed, replaced with care by three massive pontoons from Addison's speedboat.

Julia glances out the window, holding steady as she watches

the pontoon bump on the ice-covered strip that passes for a runway. "This is insane."

A large paw lands on her shoulder that she seems to think was Nausica's until she realizes he's now filming me. "Isn't it awesome?" Addison breathes. "So sorry I didn't have a second rocket." The bear squeezes the leopard's shoulder and Julia's paw comes up to cover his.

I see all this spontaneous danger-driven affection, but decide I shouldn't be jealous. In the adrenaline rush that proceeds every show, I am far too euphoric for such petty animal concerns as envy in another's joy. Also, I'm on camera and immaculate zen is kinda the vibe I need to project, right?

The song begins and we all hear the first squirrelly notes through the cabin speakers as well as echoed outside from the massive speakers on the wings. Julia totters over in front of my makeshift stage. "This is Julia Braun of Spinlist News reporting from the cabin of the private plane of internationally infamous electronic recording star Vanillupus. To those watching from the Billy-Goat Graham Civic Auditorium in San Francisco, or will be watching anyway, mark that for deletion with cut-in footage Naus—Ahem, we have a special treat. Vanillupus has teamed up with world renowned daredevil Addison Bruinster Sinclair." The bear leans in, thick paw forming a peace sign. "To break a world record of incredible engineering ingenuity in one of the coldest places on earth."

A penguin pops into frame to Julia's left. "Welding werk by Jinny!"

I put a delay on the start of the drums, looping the opening again.

"Coming up on the drop!" Jack calls back. "Everybody brace!"

The cabin has picked up speed, and the penguins are already seated and buckled. Addison settles in front of them, Julia across the thin isle and Nausica leans down so he can still film me. My performance chair comes complete with a seatbelt for turbulence so I'm fine as the drums cue up slowly.

The runway runs out, and the plane, rather than lifting with all its bound-on weight, soars off its glacial ledge and splashes down on its pontoons, dipping low and then rising fast enough to put us in the air for a second. The plane's engines are pulling us forward, but on the frozen water's surface, like the pontoon boat that Addison blew up. The drums kick in at the precise moment we all realize we're not gonna die.

One glance out of the port side reveals the penguins hopping up and down by the water's edge in the distance, waving us off. Damn, I could have played all the profanity I wanted, chicks would have been too far away to hear it. Oh well, when they play this in San Fran they'll want the good stuff kept till later.

"We're okay," Jack calls back from the front. "I have a rosary to loan if anybody needs one."

"What if you're Jewish?" Nausica grunts, trying to hold on with one hand while keeping the camera level.

The plane dodges a small ice floe. "We're coming up on the crack. Looks like the shelf is just holding together."

"Sweet!" The programmed drum kits are battling for supremacy and everyone's foot is tapping even though they're clearly afraid to die. Just like any rave worth going to. On my right is a knob set to two that goes up to twenty. "Anybody with earplugs, forget it. They won't do a damn thing," I howl and start the upturn.

The music cranks up and up, hitting max volume, rattling the plane's fuselage as a torrent of pure sonic fury bombards the spot where a rocket boat badly cracked the already displaced ice-sheet. My mouth is open so my teeth don't shatter against one another. Somebody hollers, I can't tell who.

The light comes on in the cockpit. I squint ahead to where Nathan is giving a thumbs up with one paw and wrapping his other arm around both ears.

Everybody turns to the video feed of the nose mounted camera, shuddering up and down on the incredible sonic eddy. Ice pellets shudder down the side of the glacier's crack as bits of crystalline barrier spiderweb and fall away, bit by bit. The scene blurs incredibly as the bass bottoms out and with a gargantuan shake, a massive swath of ice succumbs to stress and gravity and sonic awesomeness, tumbling with splashes into the frigid water below. The sub cuts out as the speakers blow like stunt cannons, ending the show abruptly. A blizzard of disturbed ice crystals clear, and a wide swath of empty space is revealed, marked at one jagged glacier peak by the distinct shape of an igloo cut in half. A blue feathered toucan in a parka with his feathered fingers jammed in his ears leans out with a glare. One limb extends and flips us off.

The penguins chirping through the tinnitus. "Ya done cracked the passage open, doggo! Ya pissed off old Larry but he borrowed our snowmobile three months back and never returned it so heck wit 'im. Dat's his summer place."

Julia's tail lashes as she peers over Nausica, who pans to film it. "It's slushier than a margarita machine out there. We actually did it!"

"Did anybody record that video?" I shout.

"Nope," Jack shouts from the cockpit. "It looked really impressive though, right."

"Yeah," adds Nathan.

"What, did somebody get a photo at least?" I can't believe this.

"Damn," Nausica mutters. "Sorry."

"Whatever!" Addison roars. "Guinness Book, I'm taking a page out of you one way or the other!" The bear lifts Julia clean off the floor before kissing her on the lips. Bear and leopardess melt into one another's eyes for a moment before the daredevil puts the TV star anchor down.

Julia takes her post back in front of me as I get something out of luggage, a portable Bluetooth speaker branded with my likeness that will be out for retail sale with my next album. I link it up and start a thrumming club track about all the real reasons weasels love eggs. Jack has told me it's both derisive and delightful and his parents have apparently made it their ring tone which has scandalized him to no end.

"So, we've done it, broken a glacier in half, though admittedly it was badly fractured to begin with, using pure sound on a hot dance track from North America's premier electronic wizard, Vanillupus and the mad skills of Addison Bruin Sinclair, who can be confirmed is one hell of a kisser."

Julia winks and I find my ears burn with jealousy. What am I, a defective shop vac? No, space dog, you must purge all jealous thoughts from this shared atmosphere. The resentment it brings is like drinking ipecac and expecting someone else to throw up. I finish two more tracks as drinks are passed out by Nathan coming back from the cockpit, or bridge as we are technically a luxury yacht now, and call for the first encore.

Julia looks back into the camera to finish her bit. "And Jinny the welder!"

I cough. "So, just seven hours through this passage to the next port where we can pick up a drink or two before we roll south. Hope we've got enough appetizers and ice cream packed to make it."

"We should be fine, sir," Nathan calls back brightly.

"And how about everyone else?" The others are passing out champagne flutes and we toast long life and good welding. Julia has Addison's eye and I sit myself on the starboard couch next to the leopardess. "So we'll all need to keep warm tonight. Well, the penguins will be okay, but we—"

"I think tonight we should change things up, assuming we're talking about what you're talking about." Julia checks her phone to see if she has reception yet and then puts it away.

I shrug, the booze giving me a pleasant sense of detachment combined with erotic fuzz. "Well, I can't blame you. Hey, you've got not one but three eligible bachelors ready to serve your needs. What more could a girl want?"

Julia's eyes look distant. She's smiling thinly. "I'm thinking I can use a little girl time."

It takes me a second to realize what she means. "So sorry you're stuck with a plane full of males." I smile sympathetically.

"Wow," Julia gives me a look of pity. "You're just so full of yourself you just miss *everything*." She pads off past my kit, to the bedroom door at back, leopard's tail swatting back in forth in what seems like annoyance.

Addison sits patiently by, having the last sip of a single malt. I huff. "Women, Addie. They'll never understand people like us. Rugged adventurist Marlborough mammals who live life to the fullest."

Addison frowns down at me. "Women who live life to the fullest will never understand men who can't see them doing just that."

"If such a woman exists," I chuckle and sip my drink. "I'd surely drink to her."

Addison takes the drink from my paw and downs it in one swallow. "Cute as it is, you are so damn dense, aren't you?"

"Uhh, no?" What the hell did I do now?

"Did you even know that I'm a woman? You really have no clue, do you?"

The dawn comes. Not the literal one, it's like dusk all the time this far north. "I never thought, I never noticed, um. Wow. I'm sure I woulda found out, but wow."

"Found out how?" Her great arms fold.

"Well, I'm really charming, I'm omni-sexual with incredible stamina, and we're on a plane for two days full of booze and appetizers. I'm a little bit curious about the penguins too, but I don't know what they're into."

"Don't you have more shows to do?"

"Life's a show for me, Addie. Little breaks between sets when I live as loudly as I can and set the world on fire with musical matches that I carry in my heart for—"

"If I hit you hard enough, will you shut up?" Addison chugs her scotch and rumbles a laugh.

"No, but I'll say flattering things. You might like some of them."

"Play more music, rockstar. I've got plenty of time to make up my own mind what I like. So far, it's this scotch."

"See, you drinking scotch—"

"Stop digging yourself deeper, Van."

"Really though, you didn't know Addison was a woman?" Nausica laughs in a bray. "I mean, what were you expecting, a daredevil in a pink dress?"

"Yeah, Vannie, dats a bit o' stereotippin' yoo dooin' der."

My ears are back. "Oh God, everybody, I'm sorry, alright? I don't mean to make these kinds of mistakes. I'm a good guy, really. Handsome, innovative definitely, but trying to be humble. It's just hard for me to figure things out when I get confused. These days, that's practically all the time."

The cabin goes silent. I shrink under seven gazes, including two silhouettes glaring back from the open cockpit. "You're a work in progress, that's for damn sure," Julia says with a hiss from the door to the bed cabin, tail lashing.

I frown. "I just need a chance to fix my mistakes, learn to be a better person, just maybe not brag about it when it inevitably happens." I take an extremely humble breath. "I'm-I'm sorry that I'm a total dick. I don't deserve you guys."

The cabin goes quiet. Save the tinnitus hum and seven amused sighs. Addision chuffs. "You can only get so far being cute in life."

"I'm too cu—I mean, yeah. You're right."

"And you need to think harder about what you say," Nausica rumbles

"I'll do that."

"And learn people's names if you're going to proposition them for sex," Julia chides.

"That could work. I mean, that's the right thing to do."

"Now entertain us," Jinny says and claps his flippers.

I smile weakly, my tail gratefully tucked out of sight so the whole world won't see it between my legs. "Okay, let's do this." Nausica runs the locked off camera and films the rest of my set, echoes of EDM shaking away the encroaching arctic haze. I've soon drank to the point where I won't remember much in the morning, probably wondering if I hired the penguins as masseuses or something. But then as the haze comes off I'll remember my promise, to be a better blue-furred globe-crossing artistic husky one who won't let an important moment slip by again when my friends are depending on me and it's all on the line.

***

The party carries on long into the night, eventually moving back into my room. I have one last thought as I drift off into slumber with Jack and Nathan as little spoons and both of us in a horse and bear's arms.

Julia is in here somewhere, penguins snuggling on either side of her, and says that same thought aloud. "Who's driving this boat?"

Details, I think with a shrug and fall asleep.

The Gaucho

Corgi W

Tres Lagos, Argentina

The gaucho had come far, traveling through the Brazilian rain-forests, across the Chilean mountains, passing through the tropics and some of the largest cities in South America. Now, he was here. The sun of the Patagonian Desert hid behind rolling thick grey clouds. A night when water struck the Argentinian desert was rare.

The bobcat had worked his way past the hard bit. He'd climbed to the top of the villa wall and managed to squat atop it. He scanned the ground below, looking for somewhere he could jump down. He considered his choice with care, until his eyes shot open. The tile beneath him slipped away and he fell forward. In an instant, he found himself laying in a bed of leaves and grass. "Damn," he murmured, letting out a long, reluctant sigh.

Sometimes he wondered if it was worth it. He was a rough and tumble bobcat who could put up with anything. Back in the village, there were several hassle-free ladies who liked him. He was, by his own admission at least, not a terrible bobcat to wind up in bed with. If he wanted to settle, he could. Yet here he was, hopping fences, climbing up hills, jumping about like a youth hiding from his parents.

There was a single window he wanted. Sometimes the shutters were closed, and he would have to wait for a while, until he saw signs of them opening. Tonight, though, a dim glow came through it.

He grabbed a pebble and chucked it at the glass. No response. Looking around, he found something slightly larger, which he threw harder. It made a hearty thwack. Only then did the bobcat worry about breaking the glass. After still no response, the gaucho bent down and found a stone the size of his paw. He pulled his arm back, ready to throw, when the glass panes parted, revealing the long brown muzzle of a coyote.

"What the hell do you think you're doing?" asked the canine, his golden eyes narrowed on the bobcat. "Why are you here?"

"Bored."

"That's no excuse."

"And I'll bet you're bored too, Luc."

The coyote was silent for a moment. "It doesn't matter. Get out of here."

"Hang on a sec. There's a dance on. I thought it might do you some good. Get out of that place, dress up, get down the hill. It won't be like last time, I promise."

"I'm busy," said Luc.

"Just one round of tequila and a single quick dance. That's all I want, and don't tell me it's not what you want."

"It's not about what I want. I told you; we can't get away with this anymore. Father is already suspicious after last time."

"I heard," said the bobcat. "News around town is that your daddy's getting you a bride sooner than expected."

"And why is that?"

The bobcat chuckled. "Because you're stupid. I told you to get back, but you insisted, one more cuddle, one more drink, and before you know it, it's the crack-o-dawn."

Luc gave off a low frustrated growl. "Well then, I'm going to have to stop being stupid, aren't I?"

"Now, hang– I didn't mean it like that. Hey, wait. Just one dance and a drink, then we'll get you back here before daddy knows you were gone."

The windows smacked shut. The gaucho slumped over, his bobbed tail rubbing up against the stump of a tree. He needed to get out of the villa, but could not bring himself to care. Even once he got out, then what? Maybe it was finally time to move again, to Rio Grande do Sul, or closer to the coast. The bobcat had seen enough deserts and villas and ranches and dying sandy landscapes covered in the fossils of trees and the cracked rock bones of the earth. He was about to get up and prepare himself for the somber escape when the sound of hinges squeaking caught his attention.

"Just one drink and a dance," said the coyote.

The bobcat did not have time to respond before the coyote had vanished again. He chuckled to himself, wrapped himself tighter in his poncho, and began to weave his way across the courtyard.

***

Dusty air blew through the streets of Tres Lagos. The town rested atop a land filled with sand and bone. "Dry" was the only word one really needed to describe it. Water could only be pumped from the ground, and the feasibility of that was hit-or-miss. Anything living arrived from far away. Dirt and rust covered every scrap of metal. As with many desert towns, Tres Lagos had been built with high expectations, before becoming swiftly forgotten, left with the mayor to rule over those who could not afford to move on.

The gaucho liked it well enough. If things continued, it would likely be completely empty in a few generations: a collection of grey, yellow, and deep orange walls against a barren landscape. Until then, it served as a hub for the gaucho, traveling merchants, and other such wanderers. About twice a month, a caravan would pass through. It was one of the few times that the people of Tres Lagos would be able to buy preserved parsley for *chimichurri*, spiced sausage, alcohol, coffee, tea, and other such things. Once that was gone, one would hope the next caravan wasn't far behind. If you learned one thing growing up in the desert, it was how to ration supplies.

The bobcat sat on the precipice of his porch cleaning out his revolver, more out of habit than necessity. There was always a degree of nerviness in the wait. The soles of his feet were blistered. A few of his wounds had turned nasty, with pus-filled lumps of flesh growing beside them, which burst like the yolks of soft fried eggs. Since he was a child his back had pained him, and he had never found the time, money, or willingness to hunt down a medical man who could even claim to fix it. His paws felt the years: claws chipped, pads hard and leathery, fingers that made a cracking when he opened them too much. To his relief, his muzzle and face had remained almost unblemished, save for a slowly rotting set of back teeth and a half torn away ear. He put the gun down and picked up a rusted can filled with transparent liquid. When he put it close to his nose his eyes stung, like they were trying to invert themselves. Clenching his teeth, the bobcat began to rub the alcohol into his wounds. He wanted to look good that night.

At the top of the hill under which Tres Lagos was built, the lights of the villa were slowly waking up. He wondered what the mayor and his generals were doing up there. Searing pain interrupted any such thoughts as his paws dabbed alcohol into the fresh scrapes on his stomach. He had never had much, save for his body and he kept that as well as any drifter could be expected to. Looking down, he suspected that one of those pus lumps or ever-bleeding sores was on the verge of killing him. He had accepted it. Until then, though, he intended to live.

A small plume of dust began to rise along the winding path, coming down from the hill. The bobcat had a feeling that he knew who it was, but he kept his paw on his gun.

His fears were alleviated once he saw the tips of two ears, expanding onto a brown forehead, then into a long muzzle. He wanted to call the name of the coyote, but he restrained himself; other people were within earshot.

"You made it out," he said once Luc was close enough.

"Ye-yeah…" the coyote seemed out of breath.

The gaucho's eyes shot up to the hill.

"Nothing went wrong," Luc managed between pants, his tongue smacking at the wind. "But I wanted to get here fast. Bit out of breath."

The bobcat did not relax his muscles. When he was with Luc, every inch of him had to be on guard, his paw able to dart into his holster, his legs ready to take off. "'Yotes shouldn't run. Especially spoiled rich ones. You're not sexy when you're all sweaty, y'know." The gaucho was almost swept off his feet. Two arms wrapped around his neck, a muzzle nestled beside his ear, and a warm body pressed up against him.

"I missed you," the coyote said.

The bobcat grabbed back, gently running his nose against the canine's cheek, licking, then kissing the brown forehead. "I've thought about you every night, y'know. Hookers just ain't the same."

"Y-You didn't."

"Naw." The bobcat laughed. "Well, depending on your definition."

A paw hit the gaucho. A dull pain coursed through his arm. Luc was still smiling. Early on, they had agreed on certain arrangements. God only knew what coyotes got up to on their outings to the city.

"Should you get changed?" he asked.

Luc nodded as the pair proceeded up the porch and into the bobcat's house.

"It's under the floorboards. You can get changed in here. I'll keep my back turned. Don't want to spoil the magic." The gaucho spun on his heel, fixing his eyes to the windows.

Behind him, he heard wood hitting wood, followed by a loud thump, a chest opening, then clothes falling to the floor. A few soft grunts could be heard from the coyote. The bobcat fixed his gaze more firmly to the outside. He may have been a scoundrel by most people's accounts, but he upheld his word, always. The gaucho stood in silence as the coyote continued to pant, growl, and tumble.

"Need some help?" asked the bobcat.

"I'm fine," the coyote replied, voice already softening. "In fact… I'm done."

He spun around. Standing in the middle of his abode was a coyote in a long off-white dress, almost completely covered, breasts slightly pushed out, her curves exaggerated. It was hard to tell with her ears pinned back, but the bobcat could tell she was blushing.

"You look fine, Lucia" he said.

"No, no, no, not at all. I look awful. Just a guy in a dress."

"Nah. You look better than half the girls around here." The bobcat meant that. He had seen every tiny detail of the coyote's face, and still, he found it wonderful. Her muzzle was slightly dented on the left side, around her cheeks the fur was scruffy, and her forehead was somewhat large, making her appear fairly young. The wig she wore fell over one of her eyes, as it always did. And, as always, the bobcat told her not to pull it back around her ear, or even brush it aside. He loved her exactly as she was.

"Well, I need to put a bit of spray on, maybe clean up around my eyes."

The bobcat still had not gotten over the shock at the voice. In an instant, the coyote could switch from one person to another. "I told you, you look fine."

"I'm still dusty from the walk down."

The bobcat sighed and sat. "The perfume's in the cupboard, and there's a bucket of clean water around here somewhere."

Lucia gave a lazy, half-paying-attention nod and examined herself in the mirror. The gaucho chuckled. He had never met a girl like Lucia, not in all his travels. Perhaps that was why he still chose to sneak out like a youth, making discreet little visits to the lavish villas up the hill, longing for just a moment more with her. He looked up to see she was still examining herself, looking for every blemish she could find. Sweet smelling liquid turned into spray, covering the coyote's fur, the bottle hissing. The gaucho had spent almost three weeks' pay on that.

"Are you ready?" he asked again.

"I really look okay?"

"You always look okay." It could not have been easy for her. He was willfully ignorant to a lot, but that he could not ignore. "I mean it," he added, pushing up his aging cheeks with a smile. "You're lovely."

Though he could not see her ears behind the wig, the gaucho could tell they were turning red. He stepped outside, holding open the door for his partner to follow.

Lucia stood on the threshold, trepid, her legs almost quivering as she faced the outside world. "Do I really look right?" she asked. "Do I really pass as a woman?"

The gaucho gave a serious nod. He held out his paw. Soft leathery pads rubbed against his own. Lucia took her first tentative steps across the porch, her feet quickly hitting sand. The bobcat's hand clutched tightly. "I don't know how many ways I can say it, but yes, you're adorable."

Lucia's pace increased, ever so slightly. She picked up the front of her dress, keeping in step with the bobcat, as the two headed into the heart of the village.

***

She had another life down here. The other women from the village chatted with her, unloading their problems, saying things that they would never say to Luc, the mayor's son. The gaucho heard about leaders who would dress up to mingle with their people, but this was different. Something about seeing the coyote smiling, in a dress, able to casually say what she wished, felt right, like something essential and cathartic and peaceful had been reached. It was just for a night, but in that moment, it felt like it would last forever; at some point, they would have to go out.

The gaucho nursed the edge of his glass, surrounded by spiced scents of old tobacco smoke wafting through the air, mixing with spilled alcohol and dried wood. There was rarely anything that could properly be called a dance in Tres Lagos, but the people made do with what they could. Around the saloon, other gauchos from the farms had gathered, along with others from the village. There was a distinct difference in the talk and the mannerisms of the two. Those who worked ledgers and tills could never fully grasp the mindset of one who tended the ranches, who fought, who shot, who became tough to the desert and the near constant sun. On his own hands, he could feel the countless hours of work and toil, scratches and bruises, big and tiny, all woven into his paw-pads, which had become permanent features over time. His wrist was supple from reaching for his holster, and the near constant pain in his neck had dulled to a mere background-sensation, something that was alleviated, but never felt. He hoped that Luc would never end up going through the same ordeals.

The moon hung high. Sounds on the chilling night winds carried along the dusty streets. Inside the bar the music died down as patrons slowly filtered out. Those who stayed were either asleep, drunk, or casually talking. Lucia smiled, relaxing in the bobcat's arms as she nursed the drink that she promised would be the final one of the evening.

"It's just like when we met," said the gaucho, somewhat blankly, but with a hint of nostalgia.

***

That the two happened upon such a chance meeting still astonished the gaucho. About a year ago, Lucia came down the hill, in full dress, and wandered into the bar. It was clear that she had not given the outing much thought when several of the villagers had asked her where she came from and why they had never seen her before. The bobcat stood up from his table, wrapped his arm around her neck, and said that she was the widow to a friend in need of a place to stay. They sat together, talked, laughed, and drank. By the time the night grew old, the gaucho had worked out what was under the coyote's skirt. "You're one of the Gasset's, the mayor's son, if I'm not mistaken."

At that, the coyote almost jumped from her seat and ran out.

"It's okay," said the bobcat. "I've been known to wander. Ain't going to start spoiling somebody else's fun now. Besides, you're cute."

She settled back down, her arms quivering.

"Don't worry," he said, "I know what you're thinking. You're scared that if I could see through you, then who else in here can?"

Lucia was silent, her eyes fixed on the aging gaucho.

"No one, that's who. Took me the better part of an hour to see what was going on. Nobody here's close to being half as perceptive as me."

"Why did you help? Earlier, I mean. Why did you say you knew me?"

The bobcat shrugged. In truth, he struggled to justify most of these things to himself. "Bored," he commented, as if that was a good enough reason for anything. He had lived long enough to recognize when one of his gut instincts would lead somewhere interesting, even if it was not always the smartest move. Through it all, he was a creature of instinct, not intellect.

No more questions came from the coyote. She allowed herself to sink into the gaucho's arm, her muscles remaining tense, resting her head on his shoulder.

"Would you like to come back to my place?" the bobcat asked.

"I need to be getting home before dawn," she replied.

That was smart. Not just getting home, but she must have known not to be taken away by strangers, especially those who knew how much her father would pay for her. His intentions were good and simple, but she could not know that, and he did not begrudge her for being wary.

"Do you need any help getting back?" he asked.

"I'll be fine."

"Are you sure?"

The coyote looked down at her shoes and dress, the tips of which were already slightly stained light brown with dust. "Maybe a little," she admitted. "Have you visited the estate?"

"Nope."

"Then how do you know where to go? It's dark outside, not easy to pick up the trail."

Again, the bobcat shrugged. "I can navigate just fine in the dark. Trust me, I've walked all over this country, no problem."

"How can I know that?"

"My life has not been as short as the rest of my ilk. I figure that gives me some bragging rights."

The coyote gave a snort. "You're arrogant."

"I've every right to be. From what I guess, the kinds of wanderers you get visiting up on that hill are all dons, their sons, and those who can track their heritage back to Spanish nobles. They're cocky because they're never in any real danger; never had somebody hold a gun to their head. But I can back it all up, you see. Most young wanderers drift into town, talk a big game, then end up getting shot, falling out in the desert, or going in any other such way that an experienced traveler would avoid. I'm seventy-three. I left home when I was twelve and roamed ever since."

"You're seventy-three?"

"Yep," the bobcat replied proudly.

"You don't look it."

"Doesn't matter. I've been living like this for sixty odd years. If I didn't know a thing or two, I wouldn't be able to say that." He brought his head down, making sure that their eyes made contact.

"If what you've said is true, and I'm not saying it is, but if it is, then prove it. There's a wall I climb on the west wide of the villa. Get me there, and maybe I'll let you come see me again in a week or two."

The gaucho smiled. "Whose dress is that?"

"My mother's," the coyote replied, almost in a whisper.

"She doesn't mind?"

"She's dead."

The bobcat nodded and finished his drink. "We better be getting you back," he said, standing up.

Luckily, the moon was bright enough outside that he was able to find the trail that led up to the villa. He let out a sigh of relief offering out his hand, he helped Lucia to stand. Truthfully, if the moon was new or hidden behind cloud, he would have struggled. Together, the two snuck out of Tres Lagos and worked their way up towards the bright, walled-off shining beacon of light in the distance.

***

After that night, several weeks passed, and Lucia did not show up in the saloon. The bobcat took to visiting there every night, hoping to see the coyote walk in. The closest the gaucho got was a faint glimmer in the mayor's son's eyes when he passed through town, unable to exchange anything, only able to look on.

This carried on for over a month. The gaucho slumped in the saloon, biting the ends of a cigar, looking into his glass. It had been a depressing month: rumors of wars kicking off, assassinations in the capital, rebels, corrupt generals, all flowing down the Latin continent. The bobcat read a newspaper dated seven months ago. The events he read could have already been resolved, another reason to find a way out of the desert.

He was interrupted by a voice coming from the entrance. Scraggy brown fur in an off-white dress walked in, her legs shaking, but moving with a clear sense of purpose. The gaucho sat up, adjusting himself, trying to look as if he did not notice. He could not stop looking at her, though. The edges of his muzzle were uncontrollably pushed upwards.

She walked his way, picking up the front of her dress and sitting down beside him.

"You gonna get me a drink?" she asked.

"Oh? Somebody's feeling brave."

"Don't tell anybody, but my father's out of town."

The bobcat chuckled. "Meaning?"

"Meaning that I have all the time in the world, tonight."

His eyebrows and muzzle sharply raised. "I'll get you a drink."

He came back with a bottle of tequila and another glass. "You like this?" he asked, putting them down and sliding the glass over to the coyote.

"It's not the quality I'm used to… but, yes, I do."

The bobcat grunted. Maybe, if he was lucky, he would get a taste of something from the mayor's liquor cabinet.

"Did you know you can tell somebody's past by dripping tequila on their paws?" said Lucia.

"That sounds like nonsense," the bobcat replied.

"So, you won't let me try it?"

"I never said that."

"You said it sounded like nonsense."

"Lots of things sound that way," said the gaucho. "In America, just seven months ago, did you hear that two dogs built a machine that can fly? It doesn't sound possible, but, hey, that's what the newspapers are saying. I believe in what I can see. Not God nor spirits nor mystics. If I can't see it, I don't care." He was forceful with his words, as if trying to cement that the conversation stopped there. "So, show me."

The coyote's confidence seemed to have vanished. Trepidly, she picked up the bottle. "H-hold out your hand," she said.

He did as he was asked. A few drops of liquid hit his pads, dripping down the side and hitting the fur between.

The coyote leaned in close. "You've lost somebody," she said, "and you've not touched another in a very long time. Look, look there, see how the drops fall down that way? That means you're—" The coyote stopped.

The gaucho furrowed his brow. To his surprise, she had been somewhat close. They may have been generalities, but they hit him. He doubted there was anything mystical in it; she was probably just good at reading the physical signs of paw-pads. Yet, what did it mean that she could see all that from how hard, how lifeless, how leathery and weary his hands had become.

"That means you're going to fall in love with a stranger who just walked into your life." She smiled and licked the drink from the paws.

"Is that stranger a coyote, by any chance?"

"Perhaps."

"And are her feet currently touching mine?"

"Hard to say."

"And is that her hand, I feel?"

She giggled. "You see. It's not as much nonsense as you thought."

"Maybe not. I hope you also saw that I'd like a coyote to come back to my place this weekend."

Lucia poured herself a drink. "I'll think about it. Let's see how the evening treats me. A night with a charming bobcat does sound like a good way to spend the weekend, though."

***

"So, I've a question. Why do you do it? Dress up like you do, I mean?"

It had been a long evening. The pair had planned to go out drinking, but once Lucia had reached the bottom of the hill, neither of them had felt like it.

"It's complicated," she replied.

"We don't have to go out tonight. I'm fine just sitting in. I can cook up something for us, and there's a good bottle of whiskey hidden in here somewhere.

"I'd rather not say-why I dress up like I do, I mean."

He was pushing a chair across the room, making a horrible grinding noise as the legs scraped the floor.

"What are you doing?" asked Lucia.

The bobcat jumped atop the chair and hit a ceiling plank with the butt of his gun. It loosened and shook. He pushed the plank away and reached into the darkness, pulling out a thin rectangular bottle filled with a sloshing golden-brown liquid. He passed it down to the coyote.

"You think the butcher's still open?"

"I…" She paused. "I'm sorry."

"Sorry for what?"

"For not being more honest."

He tilted his head like a canine.

"There's a lot I'd like to tell you, really. I just don't know how. Sometimes I lay awake, explaining it to you in my head, but when I get down here, the words are gone. God, you must think I'm a freak or crazy or stupid."

"Nope," said the gaucho. "Now, butcher's. I'll be back in a minute or two."

"You don't care?"

"Not really. I mean, I'd like to know why you do it, sure, but if you don't wanna say, that's your business." He placed his hand on the door knob.

"Wait!" said the coyote.

"I won't be gone long." The bobcat was dead-set on what he wanted to do. His eyes did not glance back to her, nor did his ears flinch when she called his name. He simply put his mind to walking, and that was what he did, as he had always done.

He returned with two large steaks. The coyote sat on his bed, staring at the floor. She shot up when he opened the door.

"Feeling better?" the bobcat asked. "I figured you needed some alone time."

"It makes me feel right."

"Come again?"

"Wearing this. Pretending to be a woman. It makes me feel good. Real good. Like nothing else I have. Being the mayor's son, having everyone expect so much of me, being see the way I am, it's never felt right. I need to get away from that. Being in another's arms, getting to act all womanly, feminine… It…" Tears were trickling down the sides of her brown-furred cheeks. "It—I—"

The bobcat took her in his arms. "It's okay," he said. "I'm here. We'll spend tonight here, put some candles on, and curl up in bed. That sound good?"

She nodded. "I've always wanted to be courted."

"Ah, I can't do any of that. I do know how to cook a good bit of meat though. You peel the potatoes; I'll chop the cilantro and garlic."

She smiled. "You're really okay with it?"

"With what?"

"With me…being how I am."

"You're beautiful, really. I don't know why you can't see it." The bobcat shrugged. "Pretty girls make my head spin. Always have." He took some herbs out of his cupboard and began chopping.

Behind him, the coyote's ears turned red.

They ate well that night, lighting a single candle, the stars and the moonlight providing the rest. It was, by all accounts, an exceedingly beautiful night. Outside, the dust and sand begun to glow white. Inside of the bobcat's house, each wall was bathed in silvers, blacks, and vibrant oranges from the candle.

The gaucho lay beside Lucia, a thin layer of quilt wrapping the two up.

"I don't want this to end," she said.

"It doesn't have to. We could spend every day like this, if you wanted." The bobcat put a hand upon her shoulders. Her hand touched his. Together, they fell back onto the bed, the moonlight shining through the windows, covering them as they gently caressed one another.

***

In the following months, the world seemed to be getting darker.

Caravans came in less frequently, and when they did, the news they brought from up north was all miserable: talk about war, scandals, or the corruption of names nobody had ever heard before. Eventually most decided simply not to listen.

Lucia kept coming, again and again. Over and over, the coyote would sleep in the bobcat's bed. But she seemed stiff and rigid and restless, until one night, instead of falling asleep, she sat up.

"I shot him," she said. "I shot him dead. That other guy I'd been with. He said that if I didn't do exactly what he wanted, he would tell my father. There was a gun in my drawer. I told him we ought to get somewhere secluded if we were going to fuck. As I pulled my dress down, I reached across and bang. Right through the throat."

"Was it hard? I don't know many young women who can say they've killed a man." Truth be told, he was hardly surprised that she had killed. Sometimes it felt harder to find somebody who hadn't, whatever the reason.

"No. It wasn't. That's what scared me the most. At first, he began with the threats, then he started trying to drag me about, I knew that it was him or me. My body took over from that point. There was no hesitation or doubt, not until he was dead. And even then, I was only concerned with how to get away with it. Fuck him."

The bobcat nodded. On the road, one needed to have their pistol ready.

"I've seen my father have men shot. Since I was a child, I've seen those he deemed incompetent lined up and filled with holes. When I had to do it myself, it was like sitting down to write, play a sport, or any other mundane thing. I can't even will myself to feel bad about it. Does that make me a bad person?"

The gaucho shook his head. "As you said, fuck him."

"That's why I'm not afraid of you. Even when we're in bed, I keep within an arm's reach of my dress. There's a revolver in there. And I know, if you ever become a threat, I won't even need to think."

That, the gaucho supposed, was for the best. He laughed, an honest sound produced from the base his throat. "You really do love me, then?" he said.

"I just said that I could kill you. I've thought about it."

"Yet you haven't."

"You've not given me any reason to," the coyote replied, straightening herself.

"Because you've never felt uneasy. All this time, we've been on even footing. Hell, you've probably had the advantage of surprise. Now I know."

"I figured it was respectful. We've been seeing each other for half a year. It was time I let you know."

"You didn't show your last man that grace. Now I know. You were never with me out of fear, you were never scarred I'd tell people about you. All these nights, you've been coming because we have something. You can't deny it. I don't think you want to deny it."

The coyote wrinkled the tip of her muzzle. "I don't."

"Then why be so coy about it?"

"This is fun and all, but one day it'll have to end. When that happens, I want you to know that I love you. That no matter who my father marries me off to-"

"You're being married off?" the bobcat interrupted.

"Yes. Every trip for the past two years has been about a potential bride. He's getting impatient. Eventually I won't be able to delay things, and this will have to end. I'll have to put this part of my life away, lock it up, and pretend it never happened. I've been preparing myself for that. Having to admit that I have genuine feelings for you only makes that harder. Much harder. The thought of leaving you terrifies me."

"Then don't," said the bobcat. "We'll pack up, hit the road. There's so many places we can go. We just have to put our feet to the trail."

"For you, perhaps. But I can't. My father will search for me. No matter what corner we hide in, he will find us. Constantly, he's breathing down my neck. That I manage to have a liaison with you is miracle enough."

"We can head north, maybe even hop the border to Brazil."

"He'll chase us."

"Well, we can find a ship, sail up to America or Canada."

"You don't speak English."

"There are boats to Europe. Spain, Portugal... Um, Italy."

"Do you know anything about those places?"

"I can learn. I'll stay," said the bobcat. "I won't leave this town while you're here. You'll see me every time you pass through. I'll be sitting there, smiling, knowing what lies beneath the man the world sees. I can't bear to leave you."

Lucia kissed him and nodded her understanding. Yet something changed in her that night. She became cold and distant, as if her body were in one place, her mind in another. It was the last time she would ever fall asleep in his arms.

The next day, she hurried to the top of the hill before dawn. Three weeks later, when he could bare it no more, the bobcat climbed to the top of the hill and hopped the fence. There was a dance on that night. If the rumors around town were true, it may have been his last chance to see his coyote.

***

All of that was months ago though.

"Jesus, it feels like forever," said the bobcat, snapping back to the present.

"I remember," said Lucia.

The gaucho could not force himself to relax. She was so close to leaving, getting married, and spending the rest of her days as the mayor's son.

"I've given it some thought," she said. "I can't do it. I can't get married. I want to leave, tonight. I don't care where we go, but if we head north, we can outrun my father. He can't follow us forever."

"You're sure?" asked the bobcat, unable to stop himself from grinning. His stubby tail flew up from its seat.

"We should leave tonight, as soon as possible. I'll change into something more suited for traveling."

"We'll make a swing by my place. Grab what we can, load it up into trunks, then set out. You have walking boots?"

Lucia nodded, lifting the hem of her dress to reveal a pair of sturdy, well worn, pointed boots.

"You're sure?" he asked.

"Definitely. I've never been more sure of anything in my entire life." She grabbed his hand as he opened the door, tugging, then kissing him on the tip of his lips. He kissed back, holding her close. They could have stood there forever, dusty grey fur rubbing against chocolate, honey, and vanilla. There was no moonlight that night. Dark clouds had gathered. Using the few lights of the village they navigated their way to the bobcat's abode.

"We'll need a lantern," the bobcat said.

"Are you sure? What if somebody sees the light?"

"That's a risk we'll have to take."

Lucia bridled backwards. "Okay. But let's light it when we're far away. If we head off north and keep going forward, making sure that the light of the town is behind us, we'll be able to navigate."

"You've thought this through."

"For a while now," said the coyote, solemnly.

"I knew you wanted to go. I always knew it." He kissed her again.

She returned the smile, but said nothing.

***

The lights of Tres Lagos began to fade into darkness, the town becoming a world of black. Lucia had changed back into her male attire: a pair of loose jeans held up with a belt and a plain white shirt. Her dress was in the gaucho's backpack. When they found somewhere quiet and far away, he would buy her a whole wardrobe of new dresses.

Quietly, the two poncho-wearing figures snuck across a pitch-black landscape, under the starless sky.

As the bobcat walked, something cold hit against his nose. The first time, he assumed it was nothing. Until another came. And another. It was picking up.

"It's raining," he said. "Maybe we should turn back."

Lucia shook her head. "We'll be fine," she insisted, continuing to walk forward. "Should we light the lantern?"

He was taken aback. Rarely had he felt the refreshing touch of rain. Tonight, though, it was cold and chilled his flesh. He lit the lantern, the flame protected by glass, and carried on forward.

The bobcat walked out in front, holding the lantern up, the sound of rain hitting against the sand. He went on his way, fighting against the elements, until he could no longer hear a second pair of feet. The gaucho stopped and spun around.

There, holding out a gun, was Lucia. Her arms quivered. Her face was wet from more than just water. Her muzzle was clenched into a scowl, eyebrows furrowed, and a snarl enveloped her face.

"Lucia, what are you doing?"

"Dig," she said.

"I don't under—"

"Dig!"

"Why?" he asked.

"I can't risk it. You would never leave town without me, and I could not risk you exposing me. I just couldn't. I want you gone and out of my life."

"Bu-"

"Shut up! Don't make this any harder than it already is."

"I thought…" The bobcat swallowed.

"I loved you. Hell, I still do. That's why I can't take the risk. Now, dig."

He took a step back. "I've no shovel."

"Use your hands."

"Can't you just let me walk away. I won't ever come back

around, I promise. Not if you don't want me to."

"That's too great a risk," she spat. "You know who I am. You know what I've done. You're the only damn person left who does. I promised myself that there would be no lose ends. When I first started dressing up I promised myself that nobody would ever know."

"Lucia—"

"Don't call me that."

"I… The… That's your name."

"No, it's not. Dig." The coyote was crying. "Stop looking at me. Stop it. Just get to it. Now."

Reluctantly, the bobcat did as he was told, feeling the wet mud and sand wedged beneath his claws, his hands becoming slippery and muddy. It took all night and what he dug was nowhere near deep enough to hide a body. All the while, the coyote stood, weeping, but never taking the gun off the gaucho. Lucia, or Luc, or whoever he had become, was not thinking. He had held the gun all night, his eyes drooping from exhaustion.

"Now take the dress out," Luc demanded.

Again, the bobcat followed his instructions.

"Throw it in."

The gaucho looked down at the dress. She had been so pretty in it. She had seemed so happy. To cover it in mud seemed… wrong. He put it back in his bag.

"What are you doing?" yelled the coyote.

The gaucho buckled the straps, then kicked the entire thing into the hole. "I suppose it's me next," he said, lining himself up before the grave, inhaling and puffing out his chest like a diver before they took the jump.

Those words seemed to scare the coyote more than it did him. Luc's hand was wavering. More tears were trickling down his cheek "I'll do it."

"Then do it."

"I will!"

"You'll need to get closer," said the bobcat. "If you shoot

from that distance, the bullet won't have enough force to fully penetrate my skull. And if that happens, there's a chance I could survive."

He inched forwards, unable to hold the gun straight.

The gaucho watched. Lucia was gone. She had crossed a point and could not come back. There was nothing left to salvage. Perhaps she realized that and simply found it harder to let go.

The bobcat waited.

"How's that?" asked Luc, voice almost slipping to the one that she used.

"Better. But a few more steps should do it. Hold higher, else you'll hit me in the shoulder or ear."

Luc did as was told.

It only took a second. He did not even need to lunge forward. The bobcat twisted the coyote's arm. Immediately, the gun came free, flying up into the air. As it fell back down, the bobcat grabbed it and leveled it at the coyote.

"Go," he said, not allowing any emotion to show on his face.

Luc was dumbfounded.

"Just leave. I won't come after you. I won't even come back into town. Just drop your bag, turn on your heel, and don't look back. Leave your stuff and head home."

Luc staggered backwards. "You won't shoot me?"

"I'd have done it already. Hole's right there."

"How do you know I won't come after you?"

"You can try."

"Where will you go?"

"Away."

The coyote could still not stop the tears. "Where?"

"Away." Unlike the mayor's son, the bobcat's grip did not falter, and his arm did not waver.

Luc took off his pack, paced backwards, then, reluctantly, spun around, and ran back towards Tres Lagos.

For a moment, the coyote turned around and looked back

at the gaucho.

"Go," yelled the bobcat, though he could not tell if he was being heard or not.

When Luc was no more than a spec on the horizon, the gaucho holstered the gun. The coyote's pack contained most of the food. There was more than enough to get him wherever he needed to go.

He jumped into the grave and took a few items from his own bag, throwing it aside afterward. Her dress was still in there. Still white and fragrant and smelling like her. The gaucho put it back inside and fastened it tight.

If he could hold back his tears any longer, he would have worried about himself. He let out a long, primal scream. He kicked the edge of the grave, then the ground, wildly throwing curses into the air.

The gaucho picked the bag back up and placed it gently into the grave, taking the same care that one would take to move the body of a loved one. Carefully, he placed it in. Then, using his hands, he began to scoop mud atop of it, filling up the hole. Placing the last handful of mud on top, he patted it flat, wiped his hands on his shirt, and turned away.

ABOUT THE
AUTHORS

Frances Pauli writes speculative fiction and has authored over twenty novels, most of which have at least on animal character or another. She's recently focused her attention on anthropomorphic stories and is fairly certain she'll never go back. Adding the many-layered aspects of furry characters and species has put the spark back in her pen, and driven her to begin her first completely anthropomorphic novel. Her short fiction can be found in various anthologies. She posts free stories, excerpts, serials and previews of the upcoming *Hybrid Nation* books on social media site as Mamma Bear, and a full list of her publications can be found on her website: francespauli.com Frances lives in Washington state with her family, four dogs, two cats and a variety of tarantulas.

Dark End is a quiet writer from the Midwest who drinks entirely too much coffee. He is the managing editor of *Heat* magazine and the *Hot Dish* anthology. His stories have also appeared in *Will of the Alpha*, and the upcoming *Fur 2 Skin* and *Purrfect Tails* anthologies. Even more stories can be found at his website at www.furaffinity.net/user/darkend and his editorial ranting can be found on twitter at @DarkEndWrites.

Madison Keller is the author of several epic fantasy novels and a plethora of short stories spanning multiple genres. When not writing she can often be found bicycling around the woods of the Pacific Northwest or at the dog park with her adorable Chihuahua mixes.

Amethystos spends too much time thinking of dragons and magic. It's gotten so bad that she only communicates with hisses, shouts of 'healer adjust,' and what could be Latin spells. A little bit of magic exists in the strangest of places, especially the furry community. If this story helped give back to the community which sheltered her, she would be honored. Originating in San Antonio, she now roosts in the wilds of downtown Minneapolis. If you would like to earn her favor, all you need to do is link her to SFW dragon stories. Never stop believing in magic!

Al Song is a Lao American red kangaroo living near Seattle. He has studied German along with comparative literature during his days as a university student, and has a great love for performing music and learning languages. His inspiration for "Tempus Imperfectum" arose from his German and Italian courses as well as an amazing German language instructor from Italy. The shy roo also has a story published in *FANG Volume 8*, and you can find more of his scribbles online at www.furaffinity.net/user/alsong and alsong.sofurry.com

George Squares is a writer formally trained in the fields of biology, studio art, literary criticism and creative writing. He currently lives in the Virginia mountains with his husband and is training to be a teacher. He is interested in the stories of people who manage to grow and develop under cultures of oppression.

Slip Wolf has been spinning tales for a few years for different studios, looking for truth, love and flattering Instagram filters that reveal an innate highly marketable multi-spiritedness and total socio-political woke transcendence that the kits and canines will find hot. His new single just dropped in the anthology you just bought so you need to buy a second copy for that friend or lover. Peace and tail wags to all.

Corgi W is a writer from England, who frequently enjoys diving into the strange and bizarre. She is currently studying towards her undergraduate degree in philosophy, whilst doing her best to regularly write fiction, cook, and get lost in conversation with the important people in her life.

About the Editors

Lead Editor
Ocean Tigrox When he's not travelling any chance he can get (or just to escape another Canadian winter), Ocean is dreaming up worlds he wishes he could visit. Author of various published short stories, Ocean is also the lead editor of the Cóyotl award winning *Inhuman Acts* noir anthology. He's also the co-founder and lead editor of the furry writing podcast *Fangs and Fonts* (fangsandfonts.com). To check up on his writing activities, follow him on Twitter: @TigroxTales.

Junior Editors
George Squares
Madison Keller
MikasiWolf

With Wordcraft as his sword and Fursona as his mantle, **MikasiWolf** has been fighting the War of the Slush since 2007. Despite the evil forces of Lethargy and Writersblock, he's determined to keep them at bay. His work has appeared in *The Furry Future*, *Gods With Fur*, *Claw the Way to Victory*, *Dogs of War*, and *Dogs of War II*. He hopes to help edit more anthologies in the near future. Currently he hides at https://twitter.com/MikasiWolf and http://www.furaffinity.net/user/mikasiwolf

Special thanks to Searska, Miriam Curzo and Frances Pauli for their help on this book.

ABOUT THE ARTIST

Lando is a raccoon who lives in a mountainside hermitage, untethered from time itself. When he isn't making furry art, he's drinking too much coffee to be good for him or watching a television program from two decades ago.

He goes by sicklyhypnos on furaffinity and @crabbyraccoon on twitter.

www.ingramcontent.com/pod-product-compliance
Lightning Source LLC
Chambersburg PA
CBHW070007260626
47159CB00005B/1702